Adam and the Reaper

----

by

Peter N. Brooks

Preface

In today's world, greed is exemplified by the rapidly increasing gap between the rich and the others. Is it this trend dangerous? Should we reverse it?

What would our world be like without greed? Would we be nicer to our neighbors, to strangers, to other countries? Would we still make war?

Is an equitable division of the world's wealth even a rational concept? With the vast disparities in environment, skills, intelligence and education we can never be equal.

Those who have done productive work deserve to be rewarded. If everyone were simply given an equal share there would be little incentive to work and get ahead.

Why should we want to be ahead? If there were no greed, would 'getting ahead' still have meaning? Would our goal become simply 'getting enough'?

And what of those who are willing to work but are unable? What about the sick, the undereducated and those for whom no opportunity exists? Should they not get a share? Consider for a moment the years of exploitation of third world resources and then ask again what would be fair?

And what of generosity, the flip side of greed? If we were to posit an infusion of generosity into the people of the world as opposed to a decrease in greed, some of the questions we have asked might be easier to answer.

With increased generosity, of course we would be nicer to our neighbors and to other countries. We would more willingly care for the sick, the uneducated and those for whom no opportunity exists.

Is not the creation of a generous spirit a core goal of all the world's religions? 'Do unto others as you would have them do unto you.' What a truly majestic concept. If this single phrase were to replace all the pages of sacred text ever written we would suffer little spiritual loss. The pomp, the ceremony and the arcane rituals of the grand churches and cathedrals, the fancy robes, the ostentatious display of wealth and power of the Pope, the archbishops and all their counterparts around the world would be as dust in the wind, irritating and useless.

Why do we need religions? Is the quest for more stuff beyond death not akin to greed? Is faith perhaps a manifestation of spiritual greed or its step child gluttony? Do people become truer believers when they lack material stuff?

Where did it all go wrong? If generosity is the key and religion's intent is to foster generosity, then somewhere along the road it got sidetracked. But by what? By vanity? By pride? By the need to be seen as God's special agent?

What really drives man? Is it to have power over others or simply a need to have more money and stuff than everybody else?

Can we be truly generous if our bellies are empty? Does being sated or at least sure of tomorrow's meal allow us to give without restraint or regret? Is giving half of what we have easier if we believe we can earn it back tomorrow? Is it not more difficult to give away half of a lifetime's earnings? Can you detect a little greed sneaking into our generosity?

Does qualified generosity explain why the churches have failed so miserably? Do not answer too quickly, for wars have been fought for lesser considerations.

So should we try to decrease human greed or increase generosity? Which strategy would be more effective?

Being generous will not ensure we will always do the right thing. On the other hand, if there were no greed in a person, would we automatically live by the golden rule?

I don't know.

My tale takes a broad swipe at greed. Having it all around us made the job easier than finding generosity worth praising.

ɪɪɪɪɪɪɪɪɪ

"Man will never be free until the last king is strangled with the entrails of the last priest."

Denis Diderot

1

The Zhari district on the banks of the Arghandab River to the west of Kandahar is one of the few parts of southeast Afghanistan considered lush, producing opium poppies, marijuana and very sweet grapes.

The three men sitting cross-legged on the rug had lived in the Pashmul area all their lives and had grown up there during the rise of the Taliban. This was the region where the Taliban had originally started as a military force back in the '80s when the CIA provided them with the arms they needed to fight the Soviets. Pashmul had last seen intense combat in 2006 when the Canadians fought a futile battle for neighboring Panjwai and had since enjoyed a period of relative calm.

The men were all under thirty though they looked closer to fifty. They had lean hard faces with full beards, their long hair covered by the traditional lungee wrap. Although they spoke in low voices, they were seething with rage. Two days earlier, their village had been attacked for no apparent reason by US drones. The official international press reports all claimed that three senior Al Qaeda leaders had been targeted and successfully eliminated and did not mention the thirteen innocent civilians who had actually been killed. Two of the men had lost their wives and one had lost two children.

Over many years of constant war, the US forces had made significant progress in reducing the extent of collateral damage. They had replaced large cruise missiles with drones that launched much smaller warheads when they were close to their targets. It was expected that the last minute review of a target by a human pilot would reduce the chance of error.

However, the US invariably paid for information on the whereabouts of their targets and were so thin on the ground they often had no way of verifying the accuracy of the intelligence they were buying. In some cases, to make a dollar, the informant would simply make up a story to fit the rumors; in others, disinformation was maliciously provided in retaliation for some ancient tribal wrong. To make matters worse, to most of the Droners, these people really did all look alike.

As a result, innocent people often got hurt and their plight invariably spawned additional recruits for the resistance. The cycle had been repeated countless times over the years and always ended badly for the occupying forces. Yet the clear lessons of history, while recognized and perhaps even understood, were always ignored in the belief that this time things would be different.

There were no Al Qaeda personnel in the Pashmul area, in fact it was widely believed there was no longer any Al Qaeda organization in Afghanistan or Pakistan. There was however a significant Taliban presence and the Mujahideen were very active in their opposition to the occupation. Most people believed the intent of the strike was simple retribution for the local support provided to the resistance.

Following the attack, word had come down almost immediately from the Taliban leadership that the desecration of their home would not go unanswered. No one had ever been able to discover exactly how the senior Taliban leadership transmitted its orders or even who the first recipient would be, yet every one who needed to know was quickly informed.

One of the men was Peer Agha, military commander of the region and the actual target of the attack on the village; the other two were Mujahideen unit commanders. They were advised that a US convoy composed of twenty-four trucks and armored personnel carriers was scheduled to leave Kabul the next day, heading south on the highway through Kandahar and would pass near Pashmul on its way to the new US base in the Rigestan desert south east of Pir Zadeh. Agha was ordered to prepare an attack on the convoy.

The road would be mined with remotely controlled explosive devices to stop the convoy, Russian made SA-33 shoulder fired surface to air missiles would be deployed to counter the anticipated drone air support and grenade launchers and snipers would be used for direct attack on the vehicles.

The Russian missiles were particularly effective against the MQ-9 Reaper. They had been designed specifically to attack that aircraft and supplying them to the Taliban was considered by the Russians as simple payback to the US for their role in supplying Stinger missiles to the Taliban when the Soviets occupied Afghanistan in the '80s. As happened to be the case with the Stingers, there were no national fingerprints to be found on the SA-33 missiles all parts of which were manufactured and assembled in third world countries.

The Mujahideen units were alerted, assembled, fully briefed on their mission. Twelve hours later the mines had been laid and the fighters in place ready for the ambush.

. . . . .

The new US base in the Rigestan desert though small by US standards was very sophisticated. It was designed and built specifically to maintain and launch drones and required little in the way of personnel. The site was chosen to offer absolutely no cover to ground forces who might try to attack and was easily defended by any one of the battle drones based there. The base was normally home to fifty of the latest MQ-12 Reapers, fifteen High Altitude Loafer surveillance drones (HAL-Ds), one hundred and fifty Electromagnetic Pulse drones (EMP-Ds) and thousands of the latest expendable Reconnaissance and Targeting micro-drones (RAT-Ds).

The Reaper was a very formidable machine with a range of 10,000 miles, a maximum speed of 750 miles per hour, an operational ceiling of 85,000 feet and carrying enough ordnance to defeat a small country. When one of these returned from a mission, the pilot in Langley Va. would hover the vehicle over a designated maintenance pad then relinquish control to a fully automated system to align and land the aircraft, refill the fuel tanks, top up any lubricants or other fluids as required, replace any expended ordinance and return it to its hangar.

On the evening of the attack on the Pashmul Village, the area was first sanitized by sending in two EMP-Ds. They detonated their micro-nukes to deliver huge bursts of very intense wide spectrum radiation, effectively shutting down any electronic equipment used to support air defense, communications or countermeasures. A Loafer immediately moved in to the area just west of Kandahar and from an altitude of ten thousand feet, deployed twenty-five reconnaissance micro-drones. It then climbed out through the heavy overcast to an altitude of eighty thousand feet where it held station directly over the village. It could remain aloft for up to four days and provide visual surveillance through cloud, fog, rain, night and dust with HD clarity.

The new RAT-Ds flared out in the night to cover the entire village, sending back live video feeds to the computers in Drone Ops in the hopes that the facial recognition software would get lucky and come up with someone of importance in the Taliban. They hovered unseen in doorways and windows digitally recording anything remotely resembling a weapon or unusual electronic equipment. Over the course of an hour they had logged thousands of images each of which carried a notation of the date, time and GPS coordinates to be recorded by the Loafer and continuously updated when anything moved. This data stream was also received and analyzed at Drone Ops and within ten minutes, the computers had prepared an initial prioritized target list for human review.

The final selection of targets was done by the 'grownups' at the CIA, men with many years experience in the analysis of intelligence and hopefully with some appreciation of the life and death implications of their decisions. The computers had come up with a possible identification of Peer Agha (probability 76%) together with indications of a substantial cache of weapons. A RAT-D was immediately sent back to closely monitor the movements of the prospective target and an MQ-12 Reaper moved into position roughly five miles out with a Hellfire missile locked on the GPS coordinates of Agha and the arms cache.

When the RAT-D confirmed the Loafer's report that the target was still on site, the Hellfire was launched and flying at 950 miles per hour would take only 20 seconds to reach its target. This was fifteen seconds too long because five seconds after launch Agha decided to go outside to relieve himself behind the house and was shielded by the thickness of several walls when the fragmentation warhead detonated.

The occupants of the room together with several women and children in the adjacent rooms were not so lucky as they were all ripped to pieces. The only good news was the destruction of a significant cache of weapons and ammunition.

Although the primary mission had failed, the collateral damage was exactly the same as it would have been had it been successful. Indeed while the press report describing the attack would not have been exactly the same, it was close enough as to not make any difference. Definitely a win-win situation for Drone Ops if not for the relatives of the dead.

The Loafer remained on station above the cloud covered village with all sensors active while the Reaper returned to base and the RAT-Ds, not being able to climb to the altitude of the Loafer, were either returned to base or caused to self destruct. From the moment Agha left his chair, he was monitored continuously by the Loafer and could easily have been killed with another Hellfire missile. However, Ops decided the Taliban would undoubtedly seek revenge for the civilians killed in the attack and Agha would naturally be involved. It made sense to defer his execution and allow him to expose his associates.

Two RAT-Ds were dispatched to eavesdrop his conversations and when he met with his two unit commanders, every word they said was heard in Langley.

As he deployed the Mujahideen they were identified and their position locked into the Loafer's surveillance system. They were as good as dead though they just didn't know it. The snipers and RPGs were deployed, the SA-33 missiles and the operators were put on high ground in defensive bunkers and the road mined and ready for the convoy still an hour away. Sitting in McLean, Virginia, Adam Hancock knew within an inch where each man and every bit of ordnance was located. The officer in charge of the convoy was informed of the situation and ordered to proceed as if nothing was known of the ambush.

As the convoy approached the killing ground, Adam flew the two Reapers up the slopes of the mountain range to the north of Pashmul and kept them outside the 10 mile range of the SA-33 missiles. He touched a button, interrogating the Loafer above and immediately downloaded the GPS coordinates of all one hundred and twenty-seven targets into his computer and made the assignments to each Reaper. There were seventy-five Mujahideen including six snipers, twenty-eight RPGs, nine SA-33 missiles and fifteen explosive devices emplaced in the road. Although a single Reaper could probably have accomplished the mission on it's own they only carried 25 Hellfire missiles and there were 37 RPGs and SA-33 missiles to destroy. On the other hand with two Reapers, all one hundred and twenty-seven targets could be destroyed simultaneously.

Each Reaper had a small clear dome mounted under the chin of the aircraft housing the antipersonnel CO_2 laser system. These weapons had originally been developed as supremely accurate infantry weapons with weightless ammunition and huge range, using optical energy to destroy a soldier's eyesight. Subsequent research had increased the power of the laser to the extent they were now being used on aircraft to replace the much heavier 25 mm GAU-10 cannons.

Adam launched thirty-seven Hellfires locking them on to the GPS coordinates of the RPGs and the SA-33s and sequencing them to arrive at their targets at precisely the same time. Their flight was close to the ground and there was no hint of their approach. As the missiles hissed into the night, Adam increased the altitude of both Reapers until all the personnel targets registered a clear line of sight. The instant before the Hellfires struck their targets, the lasers fired, flickering amongst all seventy-five men in less than a hundredth of a second, pausing at each for only a millisecond to deliver a lethal burst of energy that exploded the man's head or sliced cleanly through his torso. A second volley from the lasers neutralized the fifteen mines buried in the highway.

Death had come to them unannounced. Not a single man among them had had any awareness of the impending attack as the Hellfires outraced their sound and the lasers were silent. They simply died. Some had died instantly while others had experienced the horror of seeing their headless body starting to fall to the ground.

It was a perfect drone mission. Complete destruction of the enemy with no collateral damage and zero losses for the good guys, except for the thirty-seven Hellfires which would be replaced at a cost of $150,000 each at the taxpayer's expense.

Drone warfare had truly come of age and *Al* was getting seriously worried.

2

It is 2016 and the US is still a nation of strip malls though fewer people are shopping. Walmart has infested every part of the country where there is a dollar to be spent and is for most people the shopping destination of choice if not necessity. Many cities have effectively died from a complete lack of jobs yet are still home to millions who live in abject poverty, their condition being largely ignored in the rest of the country. It is not that people no longer care. They are simple unaware or feel they can no longer afford to care if the problem is further away than the fence around their yard.

Other parts of the country present a bleak and forbidding aspect as much of the infrastructure has completely degenerated. Who really needs to fund interstate highways and bridges when your condo is floating in sight of the sandy beaches of Bermuda? Hard times have come to America curtesy of corporate globalization and many people have discovered the true meaning of third world conditions. The vast metropolitan areas of the financial heartland still thrive and they more than ever exemplify the distribution of wealth in America, from the lowest fringes on the outskirts to the clusters of soaring skyscrapers at the core.

Outside the cities, hard men with Uzis control their tribes and are kept at bay by millions of mercenaries in the employ of Homeland Security and watched from the air by unmanned drones. In these areas, drug money is king as the lucrative business of supplying America's many addicts has finally been repatriated.

The profit margin on the sale of drugs was simply too great to allow any consideration of labor costs to deter domestic production. Furthermore, removing the risks associated with the importation of drugs from abroad and cutting out all the middle men offered one of the last real opportunities for a shot at the American dream. The illicit drug trade, financial engineering and the corporate provision of domestic security have become the major sources of highly paid employment in the US. For anyone else without globally marketable skills, the American dream is effectively dead and anger at the perceived betrayal is everywhere.

It was our own fault, for we were every bit as greedy as those who made the millions. We were just not as smart. They thrust us into this madness by giving our jobs to lower cost workers in other countries while at the same time fueling our desire for more stuff.

Americans have finally realized there really are only two classes in the US. Only two; the rich and the others; those who own the stuff they have acquired and those who stagger under a mountain of debt to support their chosen lifestyle; those who can survive without working and those who must work to survive. The difference between classes is effectively concealed as the rich now live in parts of the country largely inaccessible to the others, allowing the myth of the middle class to persist.

Private security forces are the norm, so highly paid their loyalty is beyond question. The wealthy are protected with the most modern weapons and technology, willingly supplied by the Pentagon's labs and arms contractors. Those with billions could very well be living on the Moon, as there is absolutely no evidence of their existence available to the average citizen.

There is another pseudo class who go to the office each day but produce nothing of value for the country. These are the financial engineers. Ironically, they are one of the few groups who still have a chance of really getting ahead of the game. However, for them to succeed, many, many ordinary working class people must lose what little they still have.

With the nearly complete exodus of productive jobs to other parts of the world, the acquisition of wealth in the US has become a zero sum game. There are very few win-win situations where the resultant whole is greater than the sum of the contributions. The synergy is gone. For you to make a million dollars someone else must lose a million or a million people have to chip in a buck. This is at the heart of financial engineering and why it has become the profession of choice amongst the predatory young.

Oil has very definitely peaked. All energy prices are up, unemployment is at a truly dangerous level, while at the same time the enormous public debt and the ever increasing trade deficit have pushed the value of the US dollar to an all time low. The country is in crisis.

You knew the game had been lost when US imports exceeded exports and our economists continued to use consumption as a direct measure of economic health. In private discussion the educated American who might have conceded that something was wrong was inevitably constrained from meaningful action by patriotic cries for Free Trade. What was good for GM was good for America as long as no one was making better cars more cheaply overseas. Even today, the vast majority of Americans believe that US Multinational Corporations have the well being of the average American at heart. This is surprising as one would expect that even the mentally challenged, should they give the matter any thought, would see the notion to be completely oxymoronic. It still has not sunk in that their primary corporate strategy is to maximize profits and contribute the absolute minimum to any country's tax revenue.

When America was prosperous with a strong middle class, the capital investment required for successful enterprise development was rarely obtained from wealthy individuals. It came in large measure from many small investors or from pension funds that represented people of modest means. Unfortunately, when the middle class got smaller the wealthy did not step up to the plate and this source of capital investment inevitably diminished. The nouveau riche either did not understand their responsibility or were unwilling to accept it. They were much more likely to invest in offshore corporations with low labor costs, trading exotic financial instruments that could make huge profits very quickly or simply buying more expensive stuff than did their peers. In any event, little of that capital ever found its way back into investment in the US. Instead corporate executives were paid enormous salaries even as their companies failed and their employees lost their jobs and pensions.

This concentration of wealth allowed a small group to control the media and to shape public perception. It is not surprising that they were able to persuade the public to support policies that were antithetical to their own interests. There are few Americans who would not have described 'wealth redistribution' as a socialist plot. Yet these same citizens derived many of their most important benefits in life from government programs financed by means of progressive taxation. The brainwashing was thorough and very effective.

When the Government began to guarantee the banks against failure, it allowed them take the worst kind of gambles knowing they would either make huge profits or if things didn't pan out as expected, they could still pay their staff substantial bonuses funded by the taxpayer. Raising taxes on the middle class to help the bankers was never a serious option as it would have led to a huge public outcry, much the same as was heard in 1776 when the British tried a similar gambit. No, they were not going to risk another revolution, at least not until they had sucked the very last gram of gold dust out of the public coffers.

So instead of getting the Tea Baggers all riled up over a tax increase, the Government just borrowed the money, thereby increasing the already crippling public debt of every man, woman and child in the nation and of generations yet unborn. This was a vile act unparalleled in social history, carried out openly in the light of day, sanctioned by the people's representatives in both parties, prostitutes all, bought and paid for by the corporations.

The powers that be still promote the myth that free enterprise or even raw uninhibited capitalism is somehow synonymous with democracy. When America decides to bring democracy to the shores of some foreign land, perhaps with shocking power and awful collateral damage, it really has everything to do with strategic military positioning and the control of resources. This farce has been performed so many times by straight faced actors from all previous empires, it exemplifies our willingness to accept any version of reality offered up by the Corporate System.

It is not as if there was some kind of screen put up to prevent us from seeing what was going on. It was always right there in front of our noses.

3

The US is now the biggest global exporter in only two fields ... military power and weapons. US space based missile systems dominate the skies above every nation on Earth and of greater importance, the absolutely secure lunar based missile systems ensure the compliance of most nations.

The Strategic Defense Initiative was started in the early years of the Reagan Administration with a program known as 'Star Wars' that was the subject of international ridicule. This attitude was probably encouraged by the Administration to divert attention from the equally important development of a space based offensive capability. In particular, the Lunar Based Ballistic Missile (LBBM) program was initiated and executed without any debate in Congress and there was no public awareness of its successful implementation between 1990 and 2009. One might even imagine the hundreds of billions of dollars that mysteriously went astray in Iraq just might have found their way into the lunar program.

We'll never know for sure but the money had to come from somewhere.

Massive military spending over so many years has made the US capable of projecting immense power and destruction to any part of the world. The powers that can deliver nuclear weapons have once again adopted the Cold War doctrine of 'Mutually Assured Destruction" even with the knowledge that war with the US could only result in their own absolute destruction. And then there were the drones.

The use of unmanned aircraft carrying cameras or other sensors to gather intelligence started in 1950. The drone was developed by the US military as a relatively inexpensive, expendable reconnaissance vehicle whose purpose was to enter hostile airspace and locate, track and designate targets for attack by conventional forces. They were increasingly successful, particularly after the deployment of the General Atomics MQ-1 Predator in 1995. In 2001, someone had the bright idea of modifying the MQ-1 to allow it to fire antitank Hellfire missiles. This gave the drones an offensive capability that sparked the interest of the Central Intelligence Agency.

One year later, the Preemptive Warfare doctrine promulgated by the younger Bush, cleared the way for their use across the Af/Pak border although these operations were never publicly acknowledged by the CIA. The Agency initially used the drones in Iraq and Afghanistan but their mission quickly broadened, becoming much more lethal, global in extent and completely indifferent to the sovereignty of national borders. This was a natural consequence of coupling overwhelming US military power with the new Bush doctrine.

In 2008, the Predator was replaced by the MQ-9 Reaper, a major upgrade both in size and performance. The Reaper had twice the speed and altitude, fifty percent more range and could carry fifteen times more ordnance.

Three years later in 2011, the MQ-12 Reaper had become the standard operational battle drone deployed by both the military and the CIA. Their operations were now coordinated under a joint command that included representatives from major global corporations and provided operational oversight rather than functional direction. The CIA's activities were now openly acknowledged, very extensive and employed civilian contractors for most phases of their operations. The MQ-12 had again increased the size, speed, altitude and ordnance delivery capability and took advantage of SPN's new Fractal Ram propulsion, adaptive stealth technology and the new Dilemi vectored thrust system.

The CIA were still not satisfied with the performance promised by the MQ-12 and by 2010 they had already started work on the next generation system, the Fully Autonomous Battle Drone, the FAB-D. They wanted to deploy a weapon with the offensive capabilities of the new Reaper but one that was able to carry out its complete task without human intervention. The goal was to eliminate any possibility of the communication systems being compromised during a mission. The drone would need an on-board artificial intelligence (AI) system to give it the capability of modifying its own mission profile as conditions changed on the battlefield.

The unfortunate reality was that computers are by design one of the most inflexible, rule-following and behaviorally predictable of devices. However, while intelligent behavior does not preclude the use of rules, it requires meta-rules to modify the ordinary ones and meta-meta-rules to modify the meta-rules and so on. As the complexity of the situation increases the machine must ultimately be able to create new and appropriate rules entirely by itself.

The application of this technology would allow the drones to recognize abnormal situations and instead of simply carrying on as programmed, they would probe the situation to determine and assess the degree of abnormality and then select, without human intervention, the most appropriate action to take. They would monitor real-time reports on social, political and military factors (reported or observed), analyze the information and alter their targeting database and strike parameters to optimize the outcome both on the battlefield and perhaps in the perception of the public at home. However, the scientific problems proved to be more difficult than had been anticipated and the prototype airframe was mothballed in early 2011 pending the development of a sufficiently capable artificial intelligence unit.

Today, the Corporate System and the US have very few enlisted troops or contractors in service on foreign battlefields and there is no longer any pretense of spreading democracy, nation building or antiterrorism for its own sake. The military and domestic missions are clear. Maintain US global dominance, protect the oil and gas sources and the pipelines, retain access to vital international resources and keep civilian populations docile.

How? Let loose the drones. The stable of drones has expanded with the times and there are now at least five other classes of drones used by the military, the CIA and Homeland Security.

4

Taking the pilot out of the aircraft did a number of useful things. It greatly reduced the complexity of the vehicle as a system, it removed the need to provide life support, an ejection system, an auto pilot and other human aides, it allowed maneuverability to be limited only by the strength of the airframe and not by the frailty of the pilot and it reduced the weight of the vehicle thereby permitting a larger ordnance payload. It reduced the overall operational costs by eliminating the need for flight instruction and training with their associated infrastructure, fuel and maintenance costs and the need for post combat health care and insurance for wounded pilots. When these considerations were coupled with the growing recruitment problems, the increased use of drones in combat looked very attractive.

By 2009, CS/US military operations were being adversely affected by a lack of recruits. Enlistment standards had been lowered over the years and there was some talk of the bringing back the draft. From the outset, this was a non-starter as it could never have been pushed through Congress. Corporate America had become used to having their sons and daughters stay out of combat zones and they did not intend to permit any such change.

The contracting out of support services began in the nineties and rapidly expanded by the Bush and Obama administrations providing extremely lucrative contracts for corporate interests. This lead quite naturally to similar arrangements for security personnel and ultimately for military operations. The individuals so employed were paid much higher salaries than their enlisted counterparts and cost the public a fortune. On the other hand, the corporations providing these services made even more profits.

The arrival of drone warfare finally got rid of the need for the draft. It substantially reduced the demand for personnel in the battlefield and eliminated the guilt felt by some in sending out the poor to fight our battles. Instead we now let our children go to the Langley 'office' each morning to fly the drones and kill strange people. Somehow this seems OK when weighed against the many corporate and political benefits.

By 2008 the collateral damage associated with Drone warfare had already become criminally excessive yet was for the most part ignored by both political parties and the mainstream media. When in 2009, recruitment for drone operators in the US military finally exceeded that for fighter pilots the world of warfare was forever changed.

The Droners at Langley were chosen largely for their game playing and computer skills. Blindfolded Rubix cubers who also gamed were particularly desirable because of their ability to hold many complex 3D patterns in their minds while exhibiting remarkable reaction and dexterity with their hands. A Droner working a target-rich environment needed the analytical and predictive abilities of the chess master and the manual speed and digital reflexes of a Shaolin Kung Fu adept. Any laptop computer can generate opponents that are virtually unbeatable by all but a few of the most skilled gamers. These individuals, pre-rated by their peers in extremely competitive internet combat, were chosen by the CIA for the original cadre of drone pilots.

For many of the young men and women who became Droners, the real reward was the recognition of their amazing skills by 'grown ups' and being paid to do the only thing they cared about and would probably have done just for bed and board. Very few of these young people had any interest in world politics as they already knew who the bad guys were and had been saving the US from them on their Play Stations way back when the younger Bush was doing his thing. Ironically, there were already indications that a career as a drone pilot might be short lived, not because of any threat of injury or death, but because of rapid advances in science and technology. It was inevitable that drone piloting skills would decline in importance as vastly more computing power became available for the control of any conceivable mission.

Why not use a controller who would be limited only by the physical capabilities of the drone itself? In 2013, Drone Ops computers were already pre-empting Droner control to provide greater autonomy for self defense. While flying a combat mission, a Droner would often feel the tug on his joystick as the computer took away his control to avoid an unexpected counterattack. Eventually, history would repeat itself and they too would be out-sourced in the name of efficiency, effectiveness, economy and of course, profits.

5

On a warm summer night many years ago in Charlottesville, Virginia, a gentle breeze stirred the tall poplar by the southwest corner of the house, carrying with it the delicate fragrance of magnolia blossoms and the songs of distant cicadas. Moonlight streamed through the open windows at Monticello where a man with longish red hair paced slowly back and forth across the length of his parlor. It was a beautiful room of his own design but tonight he could have been anywhere. The man's bearing and demeanor were distinguished, even patrician; he was clearly an educated well bred man of substantial means.

He had been accorded the honor and challenge of writing the most important statement he had ever attempted and the bulk of it was finished. The pithy factual bits and lightly clad demands had been the easy part as most of the significant issues had already been thrashed out in lengthy arguments with his national colleagues over several months. The more difficult task was to enclose the arguments in words with the power to catch and hold the imagination of his compatriots, irresistible words that would frame the whole and sear themselves into the nation's collective memory.

As he walked back and forth his feelings were close to panic, for his normally agile mind was betraying him. Although he could feel the force of the words struggling for release he was seemingly unable to move them to the parchment. He had been like this for at least two hours, thinking and pacing, pacing and thinking, to no avail. It was more than common writer's block. His mind was paralyzed with the enormity of what he and his colleagues were attempting. He realized that even though their cause was just, the future could impose a terrible vengeance not only on himself but also on his young wife and child.

He had been elected to the Continental Congress one year earlier and had so impressed his peers with his literary skills, he was appointed to head a committee of five to prepare the document with the understanding he would be the primary author. He had accepted the task with reluctance and a sense of humility as his associates were all men with years of experience and were recognized for their practicality and wisdom.

Hearing a faint sound behind him, he stopped his pacing and turned around. The little face peeking out from the far doorway was framed in golden curls. It was his four-year-old daughter Martha. He moved over to a nearby chair and sat down patting his thigh. The little girl hurried across the parquet floor and held out her arms for him to pick her up. She put her arms around his neck and her cheek against his chest and said: "It's all right Papa. It's all right."

He replied, "I know my little one."

He kissed her cheek, stood up and carried her back to her bedroom. For some reason holding his daughter made him feel a little more hopeful. As he tucked her into bed his fears left him completely and he realized that he and his nation were about to embark on perhaps the greatest adventure humanity had ever undertaken.

On his way back to the office he quietly opened the door to his wife's bedroom and stepped inside. She was lying on her back with her hair fanned out across the pillow, snoring softly. Her name also was Martha. She was twenty-seven years old and beautiful by any standards. For some unknown reason he had never had her portrait painted, perhaps because he thought no canvas could really do her justice. As he bent over and touched her cheek she stirred, took his hand and said, "Is it done yet?"

To which he replied, "No my love, not yet."

He smiled at her squeezing her hand gently and left the room. Shaking his head as he walked through his own bedroom and into the office he muttered to himself, "But it will be."

While he had been away from his office, another man of much different appearance had silently approached the Venetian porch outside the private entry to the office. He was definitely not patrician and hardly seemed a man of means. He was slightly swarthy, perhaps even brown skinned, possibly a mulatto. The estate was large with hundreds of slaves who came in all colors, shapes and sizes. But the man didn't look like a slave. His clothes were all wrong. They were of simple cut and yet you could tell they had been tailored for him. He was lean of build with the smooth quick movement of a predator. His hair was long, dark and curly, his nose almost beak-like.

He did not work on the estate, had never been there before and he was sure he would never come again. He had never even seen the man in the house before that evening yet he had absolutely no doubts about what he was going to do. It would be a bold gambit and he knew it would have a profound effect on history. If the others who had directed this venture were having second thoughts it was too late. He was here and he would do what they had all agreed had to be done. Besides, he liked his profession and enjoyed the work he did. He was very good at it.

He was sure the man had not yet completed the document for he had stood in the shadows behind the open door and watched his tortured efforts for the better part of an hour. When the man finally left the office, the dark figure pulled up his hood and ran down the porch steps and around to the front of the house.

Through the windows he watched the man pace back and forth, stopping for a moment at a massive mahogany sideboard to pour himself a glass of red wine. He took a sip, smiled for a moment, then put down the glass and continued pacing, his chin on his chest and his hands clasped behind his back. He seemed rapt in thought and when the little girl came into the parlor, the watcher felt a tiny bit of regret as he sensed the love between father and child. It was a relationship that he envied and one that he knew he could never experience.

Moving back to the shadows of the office porch he stood in the doorway holding in his gloved hand what appeared to be a tiny silver snake. He crossed the room without a sound and placed it gently amongst the papers piled on the desk. He glanced around the room then smiled, showing a perfect set of extraordinarily white teeth. The conditions could not have been better. Not too bright, not too dark. He glanced back at the desk and saw that the silver creature had already concealed itself, waiting to do what it did best. He heard the man returning and stepping quietly through the tall doors, stood in the darkness to watch.

Entering the room with fond thoughts of his wife and child, he sat down stretching his legs out comfortably on the red leather bench. Resting his left hand on the desk he reached across and picked up the unfinished document. The thing hidden among the papers stirred and then froze again as the man abruptly threw the document back. Placing his hands behind his head, he leaned back as if to search the walls for inspiration, but there was nothing there for him. His mind was still completely blank.

He closed his eyes and slowly lowered his arms to rest both his hands on the front of the desk. He was wearing a high-necked white shirt with lacy frilled sleeves that provided the perfect opportunity. The dark figure in the shadow of the porch smiled at the silver thing slipped inside the cuff of the right sleeve.

The effect was instantaneous. For the watcher it was always satisfying to see the play of emotions; first shock, then bewilderment, followed by astonishment and finally understanding. The man's mind flashed back to the previous night sitting on his porch swing drawing on his long-stemmed alderman packed with some particularly fine buds. The euphoria he was now experiencing was different, but it did have some of the same mystical qualities. He pulled out a new sheet of parchment from the drawer of his desk and without any conscious volition, he started to write. He was unable to stop himself and felt the inevitability of every word as they cascaded from his pen like an ode to joy.

"When in the Course of human events it becomes necessary for one people to dissolve the political bands which have connected them with another, and to assume among the powers of the Earth, the separate and equal station to which the Laws of Nature and of Nature's God entitle them, a decent respect to the opinions of mankind requires that they should declare the causes which impel them to the separation."

"We hold these truths to be self-evident, that all men are created equal, that they are endowed by their Creator with certain unalienable Rights, that among these are Life, Liberty and the pursuit of Happiness."

The words kept flowing freely and when he finished an hour later, he was no longer tired. Far from it. He felt exhilarated with a sense of complete satisfaction. He had no idea where the words had come from, but he knew the framework he had built would carry through history. It was good. It was very, very good.

As he rose from his desk to give his wife the news, *Tabor* slipped silently from his cuff, flowed down the side of the desk and darted across the floor to *Al* who was waiting patiently in the shadows.

It was June 5, 1776, and Thomas Jefferson, with a little help from two unknown benefactors, had just put the finishing touches on the American Declaration of Independence.

6

Al and *Tabor* had been around the Awareness Project from the beginning of time. They had no memory of having a childhood. One minute there was nothing and the next they were all grown up with super powers and a really important mission. They were watchers whose job it was to prevent events from happening that could ruin the experiment. They were not supposed to interfere with the natural progress of things but they did have a great deal of leeway in deciding what they could do.

Al knew they must be pretty special for even though there were others like them watching similar experiments across untold billions of galaxies, theirs was the only one that had yet shown the spontaneous evolution of self-awareness. And even though the process was only just starting the apparent uniqueness of Earth made it infinitely precious.

The real goal of the Project was the development of other-awareness, the ability of a species to share the thoughts and perceptions of others of its kind and ultimately those of all living creatures. In this regard, humanity still had a very long way to go. Since the initial breakthrough three and a half million years ago they had made little progress and shown virtually no signs of any other-awareness. Indeed their current behaviour made it unlikely to happen and could even result in them destroying themselves.

Al and *Tabor* had some unusual talents. *Al* was the planner and the coercer. He was very smart, good at short and medium term planning and absolutely amazing when it came to manipulating individuals. He could get inside your head and make you see and feel things that simply were not real. Unfortunately, manipulating individuals was one of the principal things he had been cautioned about.

The Awareness Project was expected to develop in an environment as free from outside interference as possible and changing the natural path of an individual was generally considered to be unwise. *Al* had a clear understanding of the 'butterfly effect' so he usually left such problems for *Tabor* to handle. For the most part, he stuck to his primary role as a Watcher.

In his body of choice *Al* could easily have been labeled a 'ragtop' in today's America particularly in the aftermath of the Twin Towers disaster when brown was not the most popular color to be. While it might be very attractive on the beach or in bed, it became a definite no-no at the airport. To make a bad situation worse, when people started paying a little more attention to their fellow citizens they suddenly realized there were a very large number of brown people living in their neighborhoods. 'How will we ever know who the bad guys are?' was a question with no answer. The brown scare faded as quickly as it had started when America realized it still had to have the beds made, the laundry done and the hedges clipped.

Al had spent a great deal of time talking to brown Americans, as it was such a curious group to be in … a sort of no-man's land. 'You're not black and you're clearly not white. Just what the hell are you?' It was like trying to categorize the space between Republicans and Democrats or between good and bad or yes, between black and white. Not an easy task as it would clearly require thought, a commodity so rare in twenty-first century America you would have expected some canny old bugger to have slapped a hefty price tag on it and made himself a ton of money.

Before 9/11, being brown was kind of a mixed blessing. 'Not really the guy you want your daughter to bring home but not too bad. Hey, it could be worse if you catch my drift.' These attitudes had no real meaning for *Al* as no one could see him unless he wanted them to and besides, he really liked the person he saw when he looked in the mirror.

Tabor could change you. He was a being who consisted of an uncountable number of subords, an infinite number of tiny brains each capable of operating independently yet able to merge and function as an immense array of parallel processors. He could predict the consequences of the smallest event with a high degree of accuracy and tell you if the temporal ripples would die out or become a destructive tsunami. Being able to identify those events that would certainly change history and those that would not made him invaluable to *Al* when he had to make adjustments.

Tabor could divide himself into as many subords as a job required and in the blink of an eye, he could disperse his parts to any part of the Earth. Though they all usually reassembled at the end of a mission, there was no guarantee. Over the centuries a considerable number of them had gone AWOL. This did not bother *Tabor*. He knew they were missing and assumed they all had very good reasons. His subords understood the stakes and would act independently only if they believed it would be of help in preserving the integrity of the Project.

Tabor did not like to work with individuals to create long-term changes, as there was too much uncertainty. If he interfered it has to be broadband for immediate and persistent change with less chance for anomalies. One exception to his rule was in helping Jefferson. In that particular case, he would have argued that it was really *Al's* show and he was just helping with the natural course of events.

Any observer might have assumed that *Tabor* worked for *Al*. This was not the case as it was very much a partnership of equals. When they needed to communicate, they did so by merging. *Tabor* would slip a subord under *Al's* skin and link their minds directly so that everything known to him should be known to *Al* and vice versa. For very good reason, neither knew if the other was able to block off a part of their mind but both suspected it was a possibility. There definitely were times when *Tabor* would do things on his own without talking to *Al*. He had the advantage of being everywhere he wanted to be at the same time, one of the main reasons for his creation. There had to be some way to gather global information in real time for *Al* to properly monitor and when necessary, control the progress of the experiment.

He and *Tabor* had been together right from the start and were a perfect complement to each other which is no doubt why they were given the assignment.

7

The experiment was started four billion years ago and *Al* and *Tabor* had been watching it ever since. They put a little pure life into the world then sat back and waited. It took damn near one and a half billion years for those first critters to start using oxygen and almost as long again for them to discover sex. Can you imagine a world where no one had sex for three billion years? Unbelievable. Although the sex thing did speed up evolution, it wasn't till five hundred and fifty million years ago they got around to developing a brain. Oh I know what you're saying ... first things first. Besides they were just flatworms. Forty-five million years later, they started growing bones as though having boners wasn't enough.

Another hundred and forty million years went by and don't you know it, we've got fishes with jaws, bones and brains crawling around on the bottom of the shallow ponds and looking up at the surface with big eyes stuck to the top of their heads. Fifty million more and the baby had changed and become amphibious or maybe I should say ambitious for they came out of the water and never looked back. They stayed on the land and started laying eggs, a real smart way to have babies. We never could understand why they ended up carrying them around inside them though we suspected it might have had something to do with passing along self-awareness.

Anyway, that was three hundred and fifteen million years ago. Another eighty-five million years went by and along came the dinosaurs who looked promising at the start but turned out badly. They did their thing for about a hundred and sixty million years and then for some reason, died out. If the truth be told, *Al* and *Tabor* were quite pleased to see the last of them as they were really quite bad tempered and unpleasant.

Now while the dinosaurs were rumbling around, another critter came on the scene who turned out to be the real game changer, not exactly what we were hoping for, but a game changer nonetheless. It was a freaking dormouse. That was one hundred and twenty-five million years ago when finally the real ancestor of mice and man had come on stage. Makes you wonder about Steinbeck's title.

Forty million years later, everybody is swinging around in the trees, hanging by their tails and screwing everything in sight. Another sixty million and we've got apelike creatures splitting off into chimpanzees and the others who would ultimately evolve into humans. It took another twenty-three million years for the miracle to happen.

Somewhere in Africa, possibly in Kenya, a short apelike creature with a really poor coat of fur scratched his balls and wondered what the hell they were for. He had been looking at his reflection in the drinking pool when he caught sight of his pair dangling between his legs. His hand, of its own volition, had cupped the nuts and promptly started a very satisfying scratch. He closed his eyes in pleasure and when he opened them he found himself looking directly into the reflection of his own eyes. In that moment he knew who he was.

Al sometimes wondered if *Tabor* hadn't slipped in one of his little subords to sort of help things along. He said he hadn't but *Al* still had his doubts. The creature had certainly come a long way from the flatworm, except for those beady eyes and the crappy fur coat. They all looked like they were molting. That was a mere three and a half million years ago.

Having reached this point there was no turning back. They started making tools, discovered fire, found better ways to catch their food and to make weapons with which to beat the crap out of their rivals. Before you know it, they started wearing clothes. No one really knows why but *Al* thinks the one who started it had a really tiny dick. In a very short time these critters had spread all over the place and were definitely in charge. Their brain kept getting bigger and bigger even though they weren't using much of it and their weapons became increasingly potent.

Eventually someone had the bright idea of stocking up enough food and stuff to see the group through hard times like winter. This worked out very well until one day just twenty thousand years ago, something fundamental changed. Prudence turned into greed and man became an asshole. *Al* watched this happen, recognized it as a potential problem and sent in an immediate report. Greed in a highly competitive environment is a prescription for disaster. The powers that be had an urgent debate lasting about a second, on whether *Al* should use *Tabor* to tweak the path. They decided to leave things as they were and just keep on watching. That was a big mistake.

8

When man started whacking his neighbors, it was just to get the other guys stuff; his food, land, women, goats, whatever. Sometimes he did it to ensure his survival, sometimes it was just plain lust. This went on for the longest time until one day lust took over. People started making war just to gather up as much stuff as they could, even when they could have got along quite nicely with what they already had. This was a very bad trend. As the years went by and the weapons of war became more sophisticated, someone realized there was much more money to be made from the conduct of war than from the direct spoils.

Expendable weapons were one hell of a commodity. You'd buy them from your friends who'd make an obscene profit, use them up quickly and then go back for more. So the Government had to use tax money to pay for them. Big deal. There were lots of good reasons and the pundits spoke as one: 'Don't you want to support our soldiers who are over there putting their lives on the line to protect us?'; 'Fund the damn programs and lets get the production lines moving. Think of all the new jobs it's going to create in your congressional district'.

This attitude really got started in a big way during the first World War when people like Krupp developed and sold armor to protect the boys in the tanks, then turned around and sold the other guys improved ammunition for their antitank guns. Now there was a progressive business model. World War II saw the process accelerate, as all the big boys wanted a piece of the military pie. Now both of these wars were started and fought for reasons most folk would consider to be good and honorable. There were bad guys out there who posed an existential threat to a great many people. So it was perfectly natural when we got upset, took up the challenge, had a real good dustup and killed damn near fifty-five million people before it all got finished at Hiroshima and Nagasaki.

The use of the atomic bombs shocked most people and things seemed to quiet down for a while. The industries that had been mobilized to support the war effort, were now producing lots of consumer goods, employing many people and what is more important, refilling the national coffers. While this was going on, the big boys were again starting to beat on the war drums.

This time it was the Red Peril. Galloping Communism and millions of Ruskies who wanted nothing more than to bomb the hell out of America. It seems those folk just plain hated Democracy, Free Enterprise and the American Dream. In addition, they were getting way ahead of us in building missiles to nail us at a moments notice with zillions of H-bombs. The US just had to pick up the pace and build more and better systems than they had.

This was a very lucrative strategy and was kept in play for nearly forty years until the Soviets quit playing. In Washington, the big boys knew they were now too strong for anyone to think seriously about attacking the US. Recognizing that this could cause a very significant revenue stream to dry up, they set us on the road to their first wars of choice in Korea and Vietnam.

Exploiting the alliances they had built during WWII, the US was able to muster strong international support to go into Korea and save the South from the Red Hoards. Many people died and some very good money was made. However, when it ended and they tried make the world believe that the threat to South East Asia was worse than ever, there were few believers and the US had to do the Vietnam thing pretty much on its own. This turned out to be a winner for using up ordnance. No one knows exactly how much money was made producing and delivering weapons to those unfortunates in the North and the South, but it must have been one hell of a lot. The other big change was in the kill ratio. Five million of them compared to fifty thousand Americans. It was a nice clean 100:1 ratio, not too bad.

Then, as luck would have it, we had the crazy Soviet invasion of Afghanistan. You would have to believe the Russians were just going about the same old business of using up war materiel for profit. Why else would they have spent so much time in such a God forsaken place just killing people? It's not as if the Afghans were going to invade Russia. Why those folk were so poor they were trying to shoot down armored helicopters with old Lee Enfield .303 rifles from World War One.

So who comes to the rescue but good old Uncle Sam. He slips in the back door and somehow manages to funnel in billions of dollars worth of the good weapons and before you know it the Soviets are on their way home. Now this was a good thing to do even though the arms merchants made a ton of money. It would have kept on being a good thing if Uncle Sam had found a few extra bucks to help those folk get back on their legs once the show was over.

That didn't happen because there were no really big profits to be made building hospitals and schools.

However, it would not be long before US companies got to thinking about piping natural gas from Turkmenistan through Afghanistan and down on into India, a country whose economy was burgeoning and just a-pining for a reliable energy supply. If you were cynical you might even consider that a good enough reason for the US to get in there and bring them democracy. But that would come later.

In 2002, the Shrub decided with no opposition from Congress that the United States had the right to wage preemptive warfare. They could simply designate someone as a bad guy, beat the crap out of him and take profits, not from his treasury but through the process of whacking him. These trends made *Al* realize he just might have to interfere.

A few more years went by, bringing us the pain of the Iraqis who somehow got blamed for 9/11, followed by an expansion of military operations in Afghanistan and subsequently into Pakistan and Yemen. These wars heralded yet another change in the US/CS tactics as much of the actual fighting was being done from a distance using unopposed aircraft, cruise missiles and drones.

Ah yes, the drones. They were such a welcome development. Here at last was a way to keep the boys out of harms way yet still allow them fight for their country. Come to think of it, there were a few other benefits as well. You could lose a drone without losing a pilot who cost a lot more to train than kids brought up on Ataris, plus they had to be paid, insured and looked after if they got wounded.

Drones on the other hand were expendable, another magical word for the ears of the manufacturers. Send in the drones and keep those high cost soldiers at home. The public would be happy not to have to see their sons coming home in boxes, those high costs of training and sustaining personnel would diminish and the profit margins would be better than ever. The best part ... if you needed more drones the little guys had to pay for them with their taxes or even easier, with a bit more public debt.

War had become the ultimate generator of income for some and the poster boy of dispassionate greed. *Al* was not amused and *Tabor*, who was completely devoid of emotion, found himself giving a lot more thought about how he could use Adam Hancock.

9

At the end of the Second World War in 1946, many of the armament industries in the US were quickly converted to the production of consumer goods. They were able to take advantage of the millions of shoppers who had been obliged to save most of the money they had earned during the war. Individual spending was at an all time high and financial opportunities were there for the taking. This is when the Group of Ten was established.

The individuals comprising the Group had all vastly increased their fortunes during the war, raking in huge profits from the manufacture of weapons and other battlefield equipment. Though only a few were Americans, they were all well known to each other. Their business relationships were as competitive as one would expect in such a group but they were also willing to cooperate to increase profits for all. They were simply very rich, very powerful individuals who has long since realized if they were to prosper, they could not allow even a hint of nationalism to influence their dealings.

They came together one evening in Geneva and, without anything as dramatic as the swearing of an oath, agreed to work in concert to shape the burgeoning commerce of the post war world to their mutual benefit. They communicated frequently and met every six months reporting on the progress of their particular initiatives and updating their collective strategies. Over the years, membership in the group changed as individuals died. While their overall intent remained unchanged, they realized that their ability to make sound strategic decisions was being compromised by the ever increasing complexity of the financial landscape.

After the Vietnam War ended in 1975, the ties between the Pentagon and the weapons industry had become so close, complete information sharing was the norm at the very highest levels. This included information being produced by corporate labs, defense R&D labs and the even by the intelligence community.

Real power was shifting away from national governments and into the hands of the leaders of global corporations as there was hardly a politician running for office at the state and national levels who could get himself elected without the help of a corporate sponsor. They were bought and paid for and as might be expected, their votes in the Congress reflected this reality. The acquisition, consolidation and appropriate staffing of the media had been the first step in carrying out a bloodless coup leaving the choice of national strategic options in the hands of an unelected entity known as the Corporate System. To put some measure to the incredible growth in corporate power, by 2010, the six biggest banks in the US had assets equal to sixty percent of the country's gross domestic product.

When the Group met in 2001 shortly after they had engineered the election of George Bush, the Group decided the time had come to centralize their operations within a corporate structure that, while not formalized from a legal point of view, would afford them several new benefits. At the top of the list was the complete sharing of financial information.

These men controlled ten distinct information pyramids each collecting financial data from thousands of different industries, corporations and financial institutions around the world. If they were to come together in a corporate structure and merge all their information into a single pyramid, it would be a win-win situation for them all as the value of the collective sum would far outweigh the value of the individual data bases, particularly when linked directly tc the military and government data streams to which they all had access.

They decided to construct a center where this merger could take place; a center with the very latest in communications and computer technology; a center whose location and very existence would be a closely held secret; above all, a center from which they could exercise the most extensive control imaginable over the financial activity of the entire world. They called it The Vault, hardly an original choice, but perhaps appropriate for the ultimate repository of all the worlds' financial information.

It was to be located in the Badlands of North Dakota. The chosen site was stark, barren, almost alien with jagged rock piled on jagged rock. There was nothing to indicate the land had ever been visited by anyone. With no access by rail, roads or even the trails of migratory animals, it was be ideal for their purposes.

The Vault would have thirteen levels, each covering an area of 50,000 square feet and be constructed entirely within the face of a small mountain. It took five years to complete at a cost of slightly more than nineteen billion dollars. The cost was high, reflecting the requirement that there be no construction equipment or excavation residue visible at any time of day to even hint at the existence of the project and throughout construction, the face of the mountain should appear to be undisturbed.

When the project started in 2004, the first earth-movers were brought in at 11:00 p.m. on big-lift hover platforms. Their first job was to excavate caverns in which they could conceal their own presence and provide temporary hangars to serve as unloading docks for the hover platforms. Their second job was to get rid of all the debris before morning. It was an immensely difficult engineering challenge that was successfully undertaken.

Everything the contractors requested was provided with no questions asked. All personnel associated with the construction were single with few if any family ties and recent immigrants were given preference. When they were hired, they were advised that they would be closely monitored and any disclosure of the project would result in either immediate and permanent termination or in their being zeroed out of society.

This latter threat was demonstrated to each individual early in the hiring phase and made a lasting impression on most candidates. The work crew was loyal and very well paid. At least one quarter of the construction costs went to the wages and salaries of some eight thousand men and women.

One of their prime goals was to establish a dedicated financial communications network that was fast, robust and secure. The broadband service afforded by the commercial satellites was simply not adequate for their purposes. It presented serious security problems and the service was far too slow. Because the satellites were located 22,000 miles out from the equator, the transit delay for the signal could be as much or more than half a second. This made the service useless for high-speed trading.

The satellite development was started in 2005 and by January 2009, the group had placed their own com-sats in low Earth orbit, providing completely secure broadband service and cutting the delay to less than 40 milliseconds. It gave them a robust financial network with tentacles reaching out across the entire globe. It also allowed fast and easy access to the Internet while keeping their own electronic traffic secure.

The ground based antennae were of unique construction. They employed adaptive and phased array technology that allowed them to conform to the natural terrain outside the Vault. This made them easy to camouflage and impossible to detect from the air.

The upper level of the complex was a transportation hub and because it served as the primary entry to the Vault, it became the first floor. The other floors were numbered from the top down with the thirteenth floor at the very bottom. There was no need for a basement floor as each level was completely self sufficient, sharing only a single shaft elevator for the members and their guests and the high speed security elevator.

Access to the first level was limited to an air shuttle designed specifically for the Vault. It was a two passenger aircraft of extremely light-weight carbon foam construction based on the original Predator drone and incorporating many of the flight technologies used in the current battle drones. Their stealth design made them virtually invisible as they came in through the badlands and with the new Dilemi technology, they enjoyed the vectored thrust and full hover capability needed for safe and easy entry through the small window of the transportation hub.

These shuttles were more than luxurious and were available to the Ten and their guests twenty-four/ seven. When a flight arrived and the passengers and pilot disembarked, the Vault's artificial intelligence system would move the shuttle into one of several bays, run a thorough diagnostic on all electronic systems, refuel the tanks and top up any other fluids as required.

As a consequence, there were rarely any people in the hub other than pilots and passengers. Access to the Vault elevators was controlled by retinal scan and a seven digit pass code that was changed whenever a passenger left the hub. On the return trip he would be given a new pass code after he had cleared CS security before departure. The only other exit from the hub was the vertical lift platform used for taking shuttles down for storage on the second floor one half of which was used for this purpose.

The air approach to the Vault was closely monitored and protected with a layered missile defense array that allowed safe passage to aircraft flying below five thousand feet, but only if they were broadcasting the appropriate IFF codes. These codes, generated with a Busart algorithm using a mutating genetic structure, had never been broken.

The second level was split into two sections that were completely isolated from each other. Half of it had access to the first floor and served as a parking and maintenance area for the fleet of shuttles. The other half housed the technical support staff, a weapons depot and provided space for all security equipment. Each member of the Group also maintained a personal security staff on their own floor.

The third level housed all financial activity with designated control centers for each of the Ten and provided common areas for dining and any social gatherings. Because of the vast scope of the operation and the need for transactional speed, an Artificial Intelligence unit had replaced all general financial support staff except for one or two advisors. It had reached a stage where the personal touch was now only required for those really big decisions that depended as much on military and socio-political considerations as they did on the state of the markets and the economy. However, there were occasions when the detailed inspection and modification of an individual's financial situation did call for direct human intervention.

The bottom ten levels were made available to the members of the Group to do with as they pleased.

The project was completed in June of 2009. During the five years of construction, the group had found it necessary to eliminate only six individuals and to zero out four others. However by the end of 2009, to ensure their security, everyone who had worked on the construction, finishing and equipping of the Vault had been eliminated. Their personal and financial records were expunged from all searchable data bases and their remaining assets, which amounted to some four billion dollars, were transferred back to a CS general account collectively maintained for any Group expenses. The few other outsiders who may have been told anything about the project had also been found and eliminated.

The existence of the Vault had become privileged information. Since January 2010, except for the operational and security staff, no one outside the Group and their immediate family had ever set foot inside the Vault. Those that worked there were provided with a lifestyle that eliminated any desire to rejoin the outside world, not that that was really an option.

Every major financial institution on the planet has an information network that it uses to collect data from smaller firms and so on down to the smallest operations. The Vault network had been designed specifically to handle the gathering and analysis of financial information. The Group having agreed to merge their data pyramids, their information was now transmitted directly to the CS com-sat pipeline. The system was very effective and eventually, every financial transaction from a Wall Street bailout to the debit card purchase of a head of lettuce would find its way into the data banks of the Vault.

The information was gathered, sorted, analyzed, classified and the appropriate accounts were adjusted. The exact financial status of every individual dealing with any corporate entity was known. It did not matter if the transactions involved credit or debit cards, bank accounts or mortgages, Wall Street assets or liabilities, it was all automatically recorded, analyzed and made available to the Ten. The working motto of the Group was 'The Accounts Must Balance.'

It was the intimate knowledge of the aggregate wealth of all the world's connected people that provided the big boys with the desire to get out of bed each day to find something else to grasp. At last count, they knew to a penny the net worth of six billion, three hundred and twenty-two million, six hundred and thirty-nine thousand and fifty-eight individuals world wide.

The ten men who currently formed the Group abided by a code of conduct established at the outset. They were the individuals with the greatest net wealth. They had complete access to the financial status of each other and of every other human being on the planet.

If any member's net worth was surpassed by someone further down the food chain, the Group would increase the member's balance by five percent. If he were to be again surpassed by the challenger, his temporary loan would be revoked and the interest on the loan would be paid. He would lose his access to information on the Ten, forfeit his residence and his privileges would be accorded to the newcomer. It had only happened once and, to make matters worse, the loser and his immediate family were killed when their shuttle engine failed shortly after leaving the Badlands

The man at the top was relatively young and had been in that position for seven years. His sixteen point lead on his rivals was steadily increasing.

The members of the Group often chose to live at the Vault as the communications facilities left little need to be in their corporate headquarters. Some of the residents had spouses or friends who lived with them; none had children, at least not in the Vault. Personal security was much better than could be achieved in any metropolitan area and the living conditions were anything they wanted them to be. They had every conceivable comfort that money could buy, including dynamic holographic imagery coupled with climate control that provided environments some would consider to be better than the real thing.

Each level had a well concealed backdoor allowing a resident to leave the complex in a mini-shuttle in case of an emergency. In the six years that the Vault had been open, no one had ever felt it necessary to leave in that way.

10

Adam Hancock's father Charlie was born in 1967 at Hartley manor on the banks of the Rappahannock River across from Fredericksburg, Virginia exactly two hundred and seventy days after his Grandpa John carried his bride Marie Slater over the threshold of the old house.

The Hancock's first started living there in 1849 after one of Adam's ancestors, a fellow by the name of James Quincy Hancock gambled away the bulk of the old Hancock estate. Adam's Grandpa liked to think he was the direct descendant of the Hancock who put the big signature on the Declaration of Independence. In truth, the Hancock's children both died when they were very young and though Grandpa John's line was direct, it started out of wedlock.

After he became Governor of Massachusetts in 1780, John Hancock took a mistress by the name of Genevieve Wilmington. She gave him a son and he gave the boy his name ... Charles Wilmington Hancock. Hancock's wife Dorothy knew about the child and ended up adopting him when his father died in 1793 and the huge estate was eventually passed on to the illegitimate son who lived there until his death in 1847. The estate was passed on to his oldest son James Quincy Hancock. Unfortunately, James was an inveterate gambler and not a very good one. He frittered away his inheritance and had to sell the estate as well as the profitable family business, forcing the family to move to Hartley Manor in 1849.

It was a big step down the social ladder as the Hancock estate had been very, very grand. Then again, Hartley manor would have seemed quite wonderful to just about anyone other than the Hancocks. Unfortunately, they had no real source of income and by the time Adam's Grandpa arrived in 1920 most of the surrounding land had been sold and Hartley manor had become just another large old house on a relatively small parcel of land.

Grandpa John lived there all his life and loved the old place. He met Marie Slater in the spring of 1966 when he was forty-six years old. Marie was a 25 year old lap dancer from Baton Rouge Louisiana who had a thing for older men. John was a good-looking man, with broad shoulders and a bit lanky. Though he may have seemed a bit odd to some, he wasn't weird. He just did the things he thought were right and didn't much care if you liked it or not. He had had little schooling but was well read and he made a good living running a hardware store just across the river in Fredericksburg. He and Marie got married within the year and Charlie arrived nine months later to the day.

Grandpa John was so happy he celebrated by bringing home the biggest damn Cadillac convertible Marie had ever seen. It was a pale blue 1964 Fleetwood Eldorado with fins like the Batmobile and so long the back end stuck out of the small garage the family had built beside the house in 1942. He couldn't close the swinging doors and had to keep the car all locked up 'cause of the damn raccoons. He loved his Caddy and liked nothing better than putting the top down and cruising along Caroline St. and Riverside Dr. with Marie all cute and sexy snuggled up beside him on the bench seat. It just didn't get any better in America.

Marie died of some kind of flu in 1990 while Charlie was over in Iraq and she never got to see her boy as a soldier. Even though he loved her dearly, her death didn't seem to hurt Old John too much. They'd been real close and he had never once cheated on her. He just accepted it was her time to go and was happy they'd had one hell of a romp together. No regrets and lets move on. After Marie died, the old man spent a lot more time with his grandson teaching him stuff.

His son Charlie was completely unremarkable. He was reasonably athletic and enjoyed playing baseball and basketball with no particular talent. Just your average C student who liked the girls and somehow managed to scrape through high school. He went from there to work at Franklin's Garage where they modified cars for street racing and it seemed to satisfy his social needs. He could have gone to work at his Dad's hardware store but he felt that he would have been stuck there for the rest of his life.

While he was at Franklin's, he rebuilt his Dad's '64 Eldorado in his spare time. The Caddy was a classic with very low mileage, but after twenty years with its tail end sticking out of the back of the garage, it was in need of some serious attention inside and out. It took him three months with Old John paying for the parts and paint and Charlie putting in the hours just for the love of seeing the car come alive. When he got finished it was again a thing of beauty, ready for the showroom.

In 1987 Charlie met his wife Sandra Fleischmann who liked to hang out with the guys when they came over to the garage to look at the cars. She was a hairdresser and good enough to be able to afford her own place in town. When she took a fancy to Charlie the first time they met, it may have been because he had been driving his Dad's Caddy. The big back seat had been very accommodating and later on in the year, they decided to get married.

He moved into Sandra's place which was near Franklin's garage and they were happy there for the first year or so. However, she made a lot more money than he did which made him feel like he wasn't much of a man So in September 1989, to get a better paycheck, Charlie went down to the Marine Corps Base in Quantico just south of Dale City and joined up. He went off to boot camp and was completely bummed out when the following July, he was sent over to Saudi Arabia to prepare for the Desert Storm operation in Iraq.

Charlie's tour of duty with the First Marine Division in Desert Storm was difficult and brief. His unit had to fight their way through Iraq's southern border while his buddies took on Saddam's people in the North. It was not a really hard a mission for the Marines but it had been tough on Charlie. He just wasn't cut out for the killing and the noise. When he joined up it was all about getting a respectable job and more money. He hadn't a clue that within a year he would be off killing people in some dust bowl he couldn't even find on the map.

His Division had to cross minefields, booby traps, barbed wire and trenches filled with burning oil. This would have been bad enough without the constant pounding of Iraqi artillery, the greasy smoke and the sand. Always the blowing sand. It just got in everywhere and rubbed you raw.

Some would say Charlie was lucky when he got half of his right foot cut off by a chunk of shrapnel. It was not a lethal wound but it hurt like hell and was bad enough to take him out of the kill zone. He was sent home in the middle of December with a purple heart and accepted a medical discharge with no regrets.

Charlie Hancock came home a changed man. He looked much the same, even with the chewed up foot, but he had not liked being a soldier and inside he was all beat up. He knew he wasn't very smart and now with the foot being damaged, he was going to have a tough time finding a job paying half the money he was getting as a marine. So he went to work with Old John at the hardware store.

He thought he still loved his wife but somehow the fire was gone. On their first night together after he got out of the hospital they made love once and it wasn't very good. He kept thinking about the war and his messed up foot and they never did try again. Looking back, you'd have to believe it must have been good enough, because nine months later on September 11, young Adam Hancock let go his first battle yell.

11

Adam's mother was strict with him, more like an aunt or a teacher than a real Mom. Not too many hugs or doing stuff just for fun. She always made him do his homework early in the day which didn't leave much time for fooling around with his friends from school. You always had the feeling Sandra was planning on Adam going to one of those fancy business schools where they teach you how to make money by being shifty. On the other hand, she had no patience with lying and made Adam do his fair share of the chores around the house to earn his allowance.

Adam thought she was OK for a Mom. He spent a lot of time on his own, what with both parents working all day and Charlie being away 'most every evening. He had no idea where his Dad went after supper and he never thought to ask. It had been going on for as long as he could remember and just seemed as natural as the sun coming back every morning.

Weekends were different though. Sandra still went to work at her beauty parlor on Saturday mornings but his grandfather's hardware store was closed and Charlie could stay home. This was a special time. He had a chance to do stuff with his Dad that more than made up for his not being around during the week.

Saturday morning was when they went to the Old Dominion Speedway over in Manassas to watch the cars run. It was a small track, just a plain three-eighth mile oval with the cars coming by about four times a minute They got to going pretty fast, 'cause the track had a good surface and fair banking and they sure sounded sweet. Most days nobody got hurt though there was one time when Charlie's best friend Orville killed himself. He blew a front tire, rolled the Chevy four times and damn near cleaned out the pits. They had to stop the race and the speedway was closed for a whole month.

Adam liked going there not only for the cars and the racing, but 'cause all the drivers seemed to know and like his Dad. I guess Charlie had worked on just about everybody's street ride at one time or another and was known to be the best at fixing bent metal. Most of the drivers were young and they all wanted their cars to look good and since Charlie was the man who made it happen, Adam was allowed to hang around the pits all he wanted and got to know most of the drivers and mechanics. Best of all, he had a chance to get close to the cars. There was something about the sound of a well tuned big block V8 that made him want to stand still and just close his eyes. Especially the Shelby Cobras. They were like no other car at the track. Not raspy like them foreign cars ... just a mean yet mellow sound bringing to mind the rumblings of a summer thunderstorm. For Adam, it was the best time of the week.

Sundays were not as great. His mom was Jewish and she always took Adam with her to the synagogue on Friday nights. Then on Sunday, they would have a fancy dinner at one o'clock in the afternoon and Adam had to help prepare the food, cutting up vegetables, washing pots and pans and mixing stuff. Grandpa John was always there and sometimes one or other of the ladies from his Mom's shop.

It was not much fun for Adam except for the afternoons when he would go with his grandfather down to the little stream at the edge of town where they could sit on the grass and put a line in the water. They never caught many fish and those they did catch weren't very good to eat. Yet he really enjoyed just sitting quietly with his Granda and listening to the sounds of the water. Old John knew stuff and always seemed to see a side of things no one else was looking at. Adam especially liked that they didn't seem to need to talk much to understand each other.

12

Charlie stayed at home for the first month after he got back from Iraq for though his foot had completely healed, it was still very painful to walk. In his short time with the Marines he had grown up and he quickly realized that his best opportunity for a reasonable life would come from working with his Dad at the hardware store. In the evenings, he worked part time for next to nothing at Franklin's Custom Shop. It was no longer called a garage. The owners liked Charlie and let him hang around and help out with any job he felt like. Sometimes he showed up, sometimes he didn't, it didn't matter to them. Charlie had been hurt fighting for his country and besides, he was a very good body man. So they all got something off the table.

One morning in June, 1994, he and Old John went over to Manassas to pick up some hardware supplies for the store. When they were finished with their business, Charlie pulled the Caddy into a local scrap yard where he sometimes went to look for auto parts that were no longer being manufactured. Three weeks before he had seen a beat-up Shelby Mustang that had been run over by a semi. It didn't look as if it could ever be rebuilt and there wasn't much left inside to salvage for parts. Unlike the owner of the lot who just wanted to get rid of the car, Charlie could see the beauty hiding under the rusty bent metal and persuaded his dad to put up the cash to buy it. They all agreed on $375 if Charlie would come back and pick up the wreck.

Looking back, he still couldn't figure why it'd been so easy to get his dad to come up with the money. Old John was definitely not stingy. Far from it. He was a generous guy who happened to keep at least one foot on the ground and normally didn't go chasing after hairy fairy schemes.

A week later, Charlie returned with a tow-truck and trailer and took the car back to Franklin's in Dale City. Adam was just three years old.

Charlie worked on the car every evening for the next three years putting everything he earned at the shop into buying parts for the car. It was a labor of love and when he rubbed down the final coat of wax, nothing else in the show room even came close. It was in every sense a brand new shiny black 1966 Shelby Mustang Super Snake. It had a supercharged

32-valve 5.4 liter V8 (the cast-iron Triton truck engine) and special aluminum heads. It boasted calibrated camshafts, a Roots-type supercharger with 8.5 pounds of boost and a water-to-air intercooler, all sitting on nineteen inch wheels wearing 255/45 ZR19 tires and 14 inch Brembo discs, cross-drilled with four-piston aluminum calipers. He had done a complete rebuild from the rubber up with all the care and patience it needed. It was one damn fine car and it was all his, bought and paid for.

Charlie got the license for it on Friday, fired it up after work and drove it very carefully over to Old John's house where he found his father standing in the driveway with the Caddy parked by the side of the house. When Charlie drove in he just smiled and waved him on into the open garage. It was kinda spooky, almost as if Old John had known he was coming. Fact is, since the day Charlie had picked up the wreck, his father had never once gone to the shop to see the work that Charlie was doing. Sure they had talked about the job when nothing was going on at the hardware store. John had even given Charlie an advance on his pay when some of the parts had cost a bit lot more than he'd expected, but he had never once gone down to the shop.

They had been standing around drinking Dr. Pepper and just looking at the car for over an hour when

Charlie took the keys out of his pocket and handed them to his dad saying, "Keep her for me will you?" Old John took the keys with a soft sigh and said, "Sure." Then they drove the Caddy back up to Dale City and at seven o'clock, had a pleasant family supper with Sandra and young Adam. Nothing was said about the Mustang.

Sandra had come to accept their strange life and though Charlie didn't spend much time with the boy, he always treated him kindly. As for the old man, she thought he was sweet and besides, Adam adored him.

At nine o'clock, Old John walked to the front door with Charlie, put his arm around his shoulder and said, "I love you son". That was all. As soon as the tail lights of the big Caddy disappeared in the distance, Charlie Hancock walked down to the small stream at the edge of town, sat down on the grass by the water, put his Marine issue nine mm Beretta in his mouth and blew his brains out. No one ever really found out why Charlie had done this, certainly not Sandra, but 'most everyone who knew him figured it was because of that damn post traumatic stress thingee that Charlie had caught when he was in Iraq.

The car stayed up on blocks under a tarp in Old John's garage for the next 13 years. Every six months or so he would take off the tarp, recharge the battery and fire up the engine. He would let it run for a few minutes, drain the radiator and put in fresh antifreeze. Then he would get out his polishing kit, make sure there was not a speck of dust or a smudge anywhere on her paint and back she went under the tarp for another six months. Every couple of years he would drain and change the oil, but never once did he take it out on the road. The garage had no windows and Old John kept the only key in his pocket.

13

After Charlie was gone, Sandra still did Sunday dinner and Adam and his grandfather kept going down to the stream. On one such afternoon when Adam was eight, they were just sitting in the shade looking down at the clear water running through the pebbles by the bank when Old John said:

"Do you ever wonder about life Adam? Ever wonder what it's all about?"

"What do you mean Grandpa?"

"Well, take a good look at the water down there. You see all those whirlpools where the air gets trapped into little bubbles. Well, when one of those bubbles forms, it probably starts believing right away it's special. They just plumb forget that only a moment ago they were part of something much bigger. They start seeing themselves as separate from all the other bubbles and I bet they get real lonely. So they just mosey on down through the pebbles by themselves and live out their little lives wondering why they're here. They don't know that when they finally pop they just go back to being part of the air. It's kinda the way we are Adam. All separate and lonely with a heap of mindless struggling going on. It could be your Dad's up there looking down at us right now and thinking we're all just a bunch of crazy bubbles."

Adam replied, "Oh I hope so Grandpa."

Old John was not a man to waste words. When he said something he always meant it and he would never lie to you. Even though he didn't talk much, he was usually worth listening to. He had already lived a long time, seen most of the really important stuff happen and frequently took the time to think about the things he saw and heard. He always said a person could hear a lot of stuff but not learn a darned thing if they didn't take the trouble to really listen and always keep asking why people said the things they did. Yep. Old John was smart enough.

He somehow made solid stock investments with no advice even though he was a high school dropout. He seemed to always win at the dog track and was always in the right place at the right time. Like when Adam's friend Paul fell down the well. Old John just happened to be passing by with a long ladder in back of his pickup truck. Never could explain why he was out there 'cept it just seemed right.

Now when it came to video games, Adam was the teacher. Adam's grandfather gave him his first video game in 1995 when he was four years old. It was an Atari. It let him play PacMan, Super Mario and some other really dumb games that didn't do much for his brain. It did however, further educate his already talented thumbs.

For a grown up, his grandfather was good at these games, maybe better than some of Adam's friends, but even so he was no competition for Adam. Right from the very start it seemed as if the controller anticipated Adam's every intention and made it happen. He simply never made any mistakes regardless of the level of play. Yet his extraordinary gaming skill did not seem to register on Old John. It was as if he was only seeing the talent he expected.

They had not talked about keeping this a secret, yet neither had mentioned it to Charlie or Sandra. Normally any child discovering such a talent would have gone to their mother or father to brag a bit and perhaps get a pat on the head. Not Adam. In this regard he was very much like his grandfather. He liked to just look at what he was doing and wonder. Adam enjoyed playing combat games against Old

John who encouraged him to play as hard as he could. However, because it was so easy to win, he never could just flaunt his skill. When he was alone, he would play against the computer and blaze through the highest game levels filling the high score registers with his name. He never could understand why his friends all found it so tough to win.

14

Born on Sept 11, 1991, Adam would soon have an even greater reason to be mindful of that date. The tragedy occurred on his tenth birthday and the associated images of grief and suffering were deeply etched in his psyche. The endless video loops of the aircraft hitting the towers and their frighteningly slow collapse were as real today as they were fifteen years before. It was something that Adam would remember for the rest of his life.

On the other hand, 9/11 was an un-expected gift for the Corporate System. Terror had come to the shores of America at the hands of swarthy rag-topped evil doers and offered a worthy replacement for the Red Peril.

Was the CS behind it all? If one were a bit cynical, the convenience of the timing might have led one down that path. However, it would have been a tough sell for Joe Six Pack who had just taken one upside the head and whose leader was calling for patriotism and payback. All of which led to the Whack Iraq show otherwise known as Shock and Awe. *Al* could have given you the real dope on what had happened but he always kept stuff like that to himself. It gave him an edge when dealing with humans, not that he ever needed one.

On the Monday before Adam's birthday, Old John had gone down to the Mall to find him something special. He'd been at it for about an hour when he passed a store with a lineup of kids and parents coming right out the front door. There must have been thirty to thirty-five of them with the kids all talking together as if they knew one another.

Inside the store window was a big flashy poster with a large X on a green background and some stuff about Microsoft at the bottom. The sign read: 'XBOX Is Here.' For some reason he went and stood at the end of the line and watched the ones up front getting their 'XBOXES'. Old John had no idea what you would do with an XBOX but he just felt that it would be the right gift for his grandson. When he got to the front of the line he simply said, "How much?" The clerk told him and without further talk Old John paid for it and left. It was in a plain brown carton so he had it fancy wrapped before he left the mall, put the package in the trunk of the big Caddy and went home.

15

It was a curious thing, but at the very same time that Old John was standing in line to buy the XBOX, Sandra was at the Dale City Shopping Plaza pricing flat screen digital TVs. Charlie had never been one to watch TV and when he died, they still had the 13" Sony tube set in the den. She knew it wasn't great, but the picture was still sharp and bright enough to watch the news.

Adam envied the kids who played more expensive games on big screen TVs, but he didn't complain. Although they would let him watch, they rarely offered to share. 'Hey go get your own' was the usual response. Adam would look over their shoulders and see the best moves as if they were drawn on the screen with a red marker pen. All he really wanted was to show them how to do it right.

Sandra was frugal by nature, not given to spending money she didn't have, especially when Charlie died. She was also determined to save enough to make sure Adam could go to college.

She had gone to the shopping center to buy groceries and to get a present for Adam's birthday. While she was browsing the shelves looking at the latest offerings in electronic games she came across a display room that was set up to compare various brands of AV equipment. She took a look inside and saw that there was no one there and all the screens were dark. It also occurred to her that the leather armchairs looked decidedly inviting.

It was an easy decision to go in and sit down. She laid her head back and promptly fell asleep. Half an hour later, she awoke in panic to the sharp sounds of nearby gunfire. It was coming from the big screen TV off to her right and was being controlled by a young boy who looked to be about eight years old. The screen was awash with colorful explosions as he shot down the bad guys with frightening expertise.

Sandra had never before seen electronic games played on a high definition display. She was absolutely fascinated with the skill displayed by the small boy and couldn't help but wonder if Adam could do as well. She thought for just a moment of the tiny washed out screen on his current hand-held game player and went looking for a sales clerk.

Twenty minutes later, she found to her own amazement that she had paid out $1100 for a 32"

Sharp Aquos LCD/TV for delivery the following morning. Sandra was not an impulsive person and it would normally have taken several weeks of careful deliberaticn for her to have made a discretionary purchase of that size. She had felt a little puzzled by her decision when she signed the credit slip, but there didn't seem to be any good reason not to buy it.

As she was leaving the shopping mall, she braked, made a U-turn and went back into the parking lot. She sat quietly for a moment shaking her head slowly, wcndering what had possessed her to be so extravagant. Unable to come up with any reasonable justification, she rummaged through her purse, found the bill and went back into the mall determined to cancel the order.

Heading toward the store, her legs seemed to grow heavy and her pace slowed. At the same time, the rows of stores beside her became elongated, stretching further away from her with each step. She stopped abruptly and the scene in front of her returned to normal. Feeling scared, she rubbed her eyes, looked around and moved towards a bench in the middle of the aisle. She sat down thinking that she needed a vacation much more than a new TV.

After a few minutes, she got up and started off again towards the store only to experience the same effect.

Everything seemed to be so far away. She turned to look in the other direction and was surprised to find that everything was completely normal. After looking back and forth a couple of times, Sandra decided that the TV was meant to be and without further incident, went back to her car and drove home.

16

The next morning as Old John was in the kitchen fixing some bacon and eggs, the usual blather on the TV suddenly changed. The news people seemed to be getting agitated about some breaking news and at a loss for words when the video feed switched to a picture of an airliner hitting one of the Twin towers in New York City.

For the first time in his life, Old John felt weak. He was eighty-one years old and he felt every single year. He had to sit down. He watched in silence as the long painful tragedy played out to its awful conclusion. He had never felt so drained. He could only imagine the horror of the folk in New York who had taken the brunt of the dreadful attack.

He thought, "So it's finally come back at us. A strike against our financial heartland with unbearable collateral damage." He wondered if the attackers saw it that way. He knew that from that moment on, life in America would be changed forever. Our sense of somehow being more than all others had been challenged and he was certain the challenge would not go unanswered. Things were going to get mighty unpleasant before they got any better.

When it seemed the attack was all over, he turned off the TV, poured himself another cup of coffee and went outside, leaving the bacon and eggs uncooked on the kitchen counter. He went over and sat on the old wooden slider swing and tried to quiet his mind, but it just kept turning to all the terrible things that might come from this event.

As he leaned back in the swing he noticed a flicker of silver darting across the floor of the swing and over the instep of his right foot. It brought a knowing smile to his face and moments later he felt the calm. His thoughts were now clear. The sadness was still there yet somehow he understood and the future seemed a bit brighter than it had just moments before.

It was not the first time he'd seen that flicker of silver. Old John remained where he was for the rest of the morning, going back inside at one o'clock to reheat his pot of coffee and cook his bacon and eggs. When he finished his brunch, he had a shower, shaved, put on some fresh cloths and drove up to Sandra's place in Dale City.

When he got there, Adam was already home from school and came running out the door as he parked the Caddy in front of the townhouse. He smiled at Adam and said: "Hi son. It's in the back." The package had slid deep into the huge trunk and Adam had to climb inside to get it. It was quite a large box but from the wrappings, he knew it was for him.

For Adam, the national grief of 9/11 was eclipsed by the birthday present from his grandfather. The XBOX came with "Halo", a first-person shooter game that created unbelievable feelings of power in the boy. It was Adam's first introduction to whacking the bad guys just for the fun of it and, to be able to do it on the new big screen, awesome. After the horror he had seen on TV in the morning, he knew this was what he was intended to do.

17

The flock of geese left the Oakridge Golf Course at roughly 5:30 a.m. on Saturday, May 26. They circled the course as a rather ragged group with every one honking and making a hell of a ruckus in the early morning.

A hundred feet below a lonely golfer, teeing off on the third hole, shanked his ball into the hazard running down the right side of the fairway. He swore loudly and glanced up at the sky, blaming his bad shot on the noisy geese while at the same time silently thanking his personal gods for finally sending those miserable crappers back north to Canada where they belonged.

The birds made two more circuits around the course, climbing a bit and swinging wider each time until they could be seen and heard by the early morning joggers in the neighboring town of Elma, Washington. By now they had sorted themselves out into a slightly uneven but quite acceptable Vee formation with the leadership of the flight firmly established. For many of the birds this was their first spring migration yet they had no trouble in setting up and maintaining their assigned positions. Weeks before, they had practiced this skill on the course below, running down the fairways in formation, honking excitedly, flapping their wings to no effect and leaving mounds of fresh poop everywhere for the oncoming foursomes.

They all knew the routine and when everyone was in position, the leader started a steady climb taking them on a heading directly towards Bremerton. The geese reached their cruising altitude of 6000 feet by the time they had crossed the Hood Canal 20 miles south of Seattle and were now in level flight making a comfortable 36 miles per hour with a slight tail wind. They continued steadily at this height and speed for the next half an hour, their wide wings beating with effortless power. If ever a bird was designed for flight, it was the Canada goose. It was 7:01 a.m. when they approached the area just south of Bremerton.

. . . . .

Sandra Hancock had just finished her annual trip to Tacoma Washington where she had visited with her childhood friend and cousin Ellen Darcy. It was the end of May, a beautiful time of year in the Pacific northwest. The rainy weather, though not quite forgotten, was gradually being replaced with lovely mild sunny days.

Sandra and Ellen were both single mothers and each had one child, in Ellen's case a girl who was a year older than Adam. Ellen had driven Sandra out to Sea-Tac airport at the crack of dawn to catch a 7:00 a.m. Trans US flight to Cleveland, the first leg of her trip back home. She would then change planes and fly down to Richmond where she would get a local commuter back up to Dale City. After a tearful hug at the entry to the airport, Sandra said goodbye to her cousin and pulled her bag towards the Trans US check-in counter. Twenty minutes later she had cleared security and was waiting for her flight to Cleveland. Flight 0277 out of Sea-Tac was on time and the boarding went smoothly.

Sandra found her aisle seat in the middle of the economy section where as usual, the seats were jammed together. It was one of the few situations that made her happy to be a small woman.

The plane backed out of its berth and taxied slowly across several runways until it found its proper place for takeoff. The flight conditions were good; a high ceiling, temperature 65° F, unlimited visibility and light air traffic. The pilot was experienced and coming off a weeks rest. No flight could have been more secure.

The big turbofans growled quietly and the plane started to roll down the runway. Although Captain Carlson had done this hundreds of times he always experienced a thrill as he felt the wings catch the air and start to lift the massive aircraft off the ground. Its takeoff weight was just shy of 190,000 pounds, including the 32,000 pounds of aviation fuel stored in the wing tanks. Each of the two engines developed 24,000 pounds of thrust, far more than was needed to get the plane aloft. A good pilot with a long runway could do it with just one of those engines. There was much about this aircraft to inspire confidence.

The plane left the runway and accelerated smoothly to climb at a rate of 2000 feet per minute. The flight plan took the aircraft 12 miles west out towards Bremerton before requiring a 180° left turn to put it on course for Richmond. Within three minutes it had reached an altitude of 5500 feet, an airspeed of 260 knots and had started making the 180° turn. The flight was on perfect schedule. It was 7:03 a.m.

By 7:03:30 the jet had completed half of its turn and was now climbing through 6000 feet.

The lead goose of the Oakridge flock hit the center of the windscreen, exploding the reinforced glass into the pilot's face killing him instantly. The next eight birds in the left arm of the Vee were thrown violently aside by the powerful wash of the aircraft. The ninth goose was at the same height as the engine on the starboard side of the aircraft and was ingested by the intake of the huge turbofan.

Under normal circumstances, the bird would have been ground up by the high strength turbine blades, possibly requiring the engine to be shut down and the aircraft returned to Sea-Tac. However, one of the intake fan blades had a virtually invisible micro-crack extending only a quarter of an inch across it's root. It might have been a manufacturing defect or just a random incidence of metal fatigue.

Whatever the reason, the force of the impact broke off the entire blade. The result was a cascade of blade failures that increased exponentially as another blade was shattered by the first, then more and more. In a fraction of a second the entire array had disintegrated throwing out titanium shrapnel at high speed both radially and back through the low and high pressure compressors into the combustion chamber. The fuel lines, normally well shielded from outside hazards were attacked from the inside.

The high pressure rotor, now completely unbalanced, was still rotating at 15,000 rpm and generated forces that ripped apart the structure attaching the engine to the wing. This in turn ruptured the main fuel tank and let loose some 16,000 pounds of highly flammable aviation fuel. The ruptured combustion chambers vented hot plasma into the downward rush of fuel, igniting it explosively.

All this happened in less than a second. Some of the passengers sitting behind the wing may have noticed a small change in the appearance of the exhaust from the huge engine, but there really wasn't much to see. Then the entire wing detonated and separated from the fuselage, the reaction throwing the rest of the plane into a violent sidespin.

The flash of the explosion lit up the inside of the plane and the thunderous boom punctuated the death sentence as the craft started its downward spiral. For the passengers it was like a sudden turn on a good roller coaster. Every one was still buckled in and simply went along for the ride. The only thing that was truly uncontrolled was the raw fear and panic that immediately flooded the entire cabin. No one on board believed they were going to get out of this alive. Sandra had no idea what had happened. She couldn't think. All she could feel was gut wrenching fear. Although she was a true believer she did not want to die. Not like this, not now.

The explosion had occurred at 6,000 feet. The current descent rate of about 4,000 feet per minute meant they would hit the ground within ninety seconds. This was a very long time when you know you are falling straight into hell. The fear caused Sandra to shut her eyes and grip tightly on the arms of her seat. There was a slight shimmer as something swift and silvery slipped down the back of the seat in front of her, dropped on her lap and disappeared into the cuff of her jacket. A moment later she felt absolutely serene and opened her eyes. Her sense of dread was completely gone.

She looked around at her fellow passengers with compassion as they displayed every conceivable emotion. She thought of Adam and Old John back in Virginia and the sorrow they would feel when this was all over. She almost reached for her cell phone to call Adam to say goodbye then stopped when a small boy two rows ahead turned towards her and, with a very knowing look on his face, slowly shook his head. He did not seem the least bit afraid even though the woman sitting beside him was screaming. Sandra smiled at him. He winked and smiled back. The ground came up very quickly and ended everything.

18

Adam was staying with Old John when the news came. They both just blinked, looked at each other for a moment and then closed their eyes for a long time. They hurt deep inside for they had loved Sandra a lot and knew there wasn't much to do but just go on with the business of living.

Old John had the notion that if you weren't real happy with getting out of bed in the morning, life was telling you there wasn't much point in just being there. Back in 1997 when his Dad had killed himself, Adam had been puzzled by the whole thing. It wasn't like he was seeing a whole lot of Charlie. Still, those Saturdays over at the Speedway were so full of love and just plain fun for Adam he figured it should have been enough to get Charlie out of bed real quick. Not so for Old John. He understood Charlie's emotions and sometimes when he wasn't too careful, he blamed himself. It only lasted for a few moments and usually only if he'd had one too many, which didn't happen very often. You can't go around feeling sorry when someone does something he has to do.

He had believed that Charlie and the car waiting in the garage were joined at the hip and had been a bit surprised when Charlie handed him the keys. He'd kinda figured that after all that work Charlie would have wanted a bit of fancy time cruising by the mall or at least setting it out in the showroom with a big Not-For-Sale sign, but there had been something else at play.

It had always been about Adam and when the car was finished, Charlie's life was over. If he had shown the car to Adam or given it to him at the end, there was nothing the boy could have done with it being only six. Then what? He would have been hanging around feeling Adam's happiness fade away and himself starting to wonder if he shouldn't take it out a bit just to keep everything working. No, sad as it was for all of us, Charlie had done what he had to do.

. . . . .

Old John had been doing the right thing all his life. He had started his hardware business back in '46 right after the war when many folk were still hurting from the depression and needed help getting things fixed. Old John had a way with machines. He always seemed to know which part needed fixing and spent a lot of time helping folk with their problems. Sometimes he got paid, sometimes it was just a chicken and some eggs, sometimes it was an overnight stay at a farm with dinner and a really good breakfast. It didn't really matter to him. It all made him want to push back the sheets and get out of bed every day of his life.

Times started to improve as life got back to normal and business picked up. Folk often asked Old John to talk about his time over in Germany and never learned a thing. Rumor was he got himself a bunch of medals for doing some real crazy things, but he never showed them to anyone and folk just didn't press him. Though not quick to anger, he was not a man you trifled with.

Then along came that danged cock-up in Vietnam. Didn't seem to be any real reason for it. Fifty thousand of our young people gone and five million Vietnamese killed, four million of them just ordinary folk going about their daily lives and getting caught up in the cross-fire. The politicians called it 'Unavoidable Collateral Damage'.

"Unavoidable my ass." he'd say. " Those folk had no quarrel with us. We just upped and went over there and started pounding on them for no good reason except maybe to sell a lot of bombs and stuff. All the killing and maiming far off around the other side of the world because the 'dominos were going to fall' was nothing more than old man greed stomping around in our yard."

He could still remember the boxes coming home, many of them filled with boys from Fredericksburg. Then one day, folk everywhere started getting feisty with the government. They shouted 'enough' and bingo, it was all over. Nobody had won anything and believe or not, all the dominoes were still in place. Fact is some folk were saying we'd had our tails whipped and we had to scoot. You'd figure someone would go get the folk who drummed it up, take them out back and give them a damned good whipping. But Old John knew that was never going to happen. There were too many people who were real pleased with the results. The kill ratios were more than acceptable and they had made a ton of money feeding the monster.

Old John always attended the funerals and held his head high like he was proud of their sacrifice and he would go whether he knew the boys or not. After a day like that, he would close the store and go off into the woods and sometimes not come back for a week. No one knew where he went or what he did out there. Then the store would be open again with John behind the counter, no questions asked, no explanations offered: just his usual polite helpful self.

When Charlie took his life in 1997, Old John was over seventy-five. He had moved his store twice in the fifty years he'd been in business and both times for the same reason, the smells. The first time in 1954, someone had set up a dyeing plant down the road and the stink was something awful. He just couldn't stay there with the smell coming at him all day.

So he packed up and got himself a new place on the other side of the river in Fredericksburg. It was still close to home and it smelled a whole lot better. He was never able to sell the old store. I guess it was just too small or too old for someone wanting to start a new business and the smell of the dye plant didn't help much either. He ended up selling the place for the price of the land and just about covered the costs of moving. Most of his customers followed him across the river.

The next move was for the same reason. In 1968 a damn pizza parlor opened right across the street and the wind off the river pushed the bloody garlic smell right through his place every day of the week. Old John hated garlic with a passion. He did not even have to think about it. Within a week he had rented a spot in the nearby mall and put the old store up for sale, just the property, 'cause after 22 years he wasn't about to give up his good name. So he moved to the mall and stayed there till after Charlie died.

It turned out he rather liked the move as he got a chance to know a whole lot more folk some of whom had never even been inside a hardware store, Old John got a good price when he retired in '97 and sold the business, name and all. Not a fortune, though more than enough to keep good food on the table and the old home neat and tidy.

In those days, there seemed to be plenty of money around with everyone buying and selling Internet stocks. On the other hand the folk with the money had kinda lost interest in real stuff like bricks and mortar. There just wasn't much demand for a hardware store, even one that had always turned a respectable profit. All of which meant Old John had to settle for a price that he figured was fair. The day after he closed the sale, he took a long time over breakfast thinking about his life and wondering if it was going to get harder to get out of bed in the mornings.

19

Most Droners were not sociopaths, but they certainly were divorced from reality. Although they were eager and willing to watch their missiles fly into groups of people believed to be 'bad guys', they were not really amoral, just unable, after years of playing games like Halo or H.A.W.X., to distinguish reality from games when viewed on a video display. The hunt was the thing. Who could rack up the greatest number of points in the shortest time? 'Nobody is getting hurt, that's why we have the drones. Besides, those guys hate us and want to take away our American dream. Anyway, they don't value human life like we do. That's why we're all pro-life and they're terrorists.' Hard as it may be to believe, this typified the political dynamic motivating the new defenders of our frontiers.

Flying attack missions in Afghanistan made Adam feel almost godlike ... at least right up there with the archangels ... not really calling the shots yet having awesome power. Just a twitch of his finger and poof, another bad guy was toast. He was the best and every one of the other three hundred and forty-nine operators knew it for a fact. His mission success rate was way above average and was still trending upward.

On the other hand, Adam's love for his car clearly defined him as an all-American throwback. On his eighteenth birthday, his grandfather had given him the keys to the black Shelby Mustang that had been rebuilt for him by his father. The car's engine offered six hundred and five horsepower that were, for a street car, amazingly useless. However the sound emerging from the twin Boria mufflers was a different matter as it truly defied description. If you had asked Adam to tell you why it was so special, he would have just smiled, closed his eyes and shaken head softly. Decked out in his flight suit and cruising downtown in the aggressive Snake, Adam was one cool badass dude, young, fit and handsome. An instant star on the trash circuit.

In most ways, Adam had grown up to be a normal white American male, fully conditioned to accept and expect his country's preeminence in the world and his right to consume a lot of stuff. As he got older his incredible skill at video gaming had not diminished, if anything, it had increased to an impossibly high level and was somehow a thing apart from the man.

In other respects, Adam was indistinguishable from his peers. Though his job as a drone pilot made him a bit cocky, he was fundamentally a decent person if somewhat conflicted. He knew he had an extraordinary talent, yet he did never thought of himself as being exceptional.

Outside of his job he was the average twenty-something. He liked girls and was never lonely. He made a decent salary and he liked to have a good time. However, when he walked into Drone Ops in Langley, he became the Man. Of that he had absolutely no doubt. His talent for mission analysis, strategic and tactical development and above all his operational skill on the joystick were supreme. He literally became a different person, commanding deep respect and not a little envy from his peers. While he could not abide an unfair fight in his street at home Adam did not find it a problem to apply overwhelming force to officially designated targets either at home or in war zones like Pakistan.

. . . . .

When his mother died in 2002, Adam had gone to live with his grandfather near Fredericksburg. He had had to change schools and as a result, had lost track of most of his childhood friends except for the few who had always gone to the speedway in Manassas.

Old John was not a big fan of stock car racing, but he did take Adam over to the Old Dominion track once a month.

After settling his mother's estate, his grandfather had taken care of all of the things that had to be done and, before the house was put on the market, had sold off all the furniture including the big screen TV. The day after he moved into Hartley Manor, Adam had a really bad moment when he realized that his XBOX just wasn't going to work with his grandfather's old tube TV.

In the weeks following his Mom's death, they spent many hours together just walking and talking, with Old John wanting to be sure the boy was properly settled in school and feeling secure. They had always been close, and Adam was happy to be living at Hartley, except for one thing, the darned TV.

It was Old John who first raised the subject. He had asked Adam how come he wasn't playing games on his XBOX any more. "Is it broken?" he asked. That was when Adam explained about the TV. His grandfather had never been real big on watching TV and had never even considered replacing the old 21" RCA color set he'd bought new back in '71. The thing still worked, the picture wasn't half bad and besides, he really didn't use it very often. He understood Adam's problem and thought about getting one of the new models. He even went down to the mall to see some of the flat screen sets, decided that the prices were too steep and came home empty handed.

Old John made his lunch and as he always did, poured himself a big mug of coffee and took it outside to sit on his old swing. He figured it was the best thing he'd ever built. It was about thirty-five years old, made of home grown Scaly-Bark hickory that was as tough as nails and while the swing could have used a fresh coat of stain, it was just as good as new. He'd worn out three saw blades cutting the wood.

As he sat sipping his coffee, he got to thinking again about the darned TV. The whole business was troubling him, 'cause he really loved the boy but he just plain hated throwing out things if they were still in good working order. This time Old John did not catch the slightest glimpse of the silver flash darting under his pant cuff. He only knew he'd had a bright idea and the problem was solved. He decided he would just leave the old TV right where it was in the den and buy one of those new flat ones and hang it on the wall in Adam's room. He couldn't understand why he hadn't thought of it sooner. Adam was certain to be happy and he wouldn't feel bad about throwing away good stuff.

The next day, after Adam left for school, Old John came home with a real nice 40" Panasonic plasma TV and a kit for mounting it on the wall. When he told the young salesman that he wanted it for Adam's XBOX he had been assured he could do no better than the Panasonic and that his grandson would be 'totally freaked.' Old John assumed from the young man's tone that this would be a good thing and further accepted his advice that the TV would be completely wasted if he didn't get Adam a Top Gun Fox 2 Pro Joystick to go with it. This add-on he described as 'totally awesome.' For some reason Old John was not the least bit skeptical. He did not even give a moment's thought about the outrageous price he was paying as he signed the credit slip.

It only took him half an hour to mount the TV solidly on the wall in Adam's room, after which he brewed himself a cup of coffee and went and sat on his swing to wait for the boy to come home from school. He always seemed to feel at peace with himself when he sat out there. There was just something special about the way the light filtered through the leaves of the big tree. He often wondered about that.

When Adam got off the school bus and came up the driveway, he went right over to the swing and plunked himself down on the seat opposite Old John. He said,

"Hi Grandpa, watcha doin?"

"Not much Adam, but I do have something to show you. Lets go inside."

When Adam saw the TV on his wall and the joystick on the dresser, he didn't say a word. He just walked over to his grandfather and put his arms around him and hugged him for the longest time.

The new joystick was a game changer for Adam. He could now do stuff with aircraft that had been nearly impossible with the original controller. He would have agreed completely with the salesman's description, the stick was indeed totally awesome.

Old John had worried for a while that Adam would be playing all the time and neglecting his schoolwork, but it never became a problem. Adam always finished his homework before he touched the joystick. He showed surprising self discipline for someone his age, almost as if he was holding to some unspoken promise. His grandfather was at first amazed and then just very pleased as he came to know he'd made the right decision.

Three and a half years later in mid-December '05, broadband Internet came to Fredericksburg and Old John who hadn't a clue about broadband or the Internet, found himself one morning in the mall at the cable company booth, signing up for the service to be connected at Hartley before noon. He also went to the PC store and bought a Dell laptop with Windows installed (whatever the hell Windows were) and some other software the salesman said he would need to get going on the Internet.

He brought the computer home and put it away in his bedroom closet and didn't say anything to Adam. That was in mid December. On Christmas Eve, before he went to bed, he got out the computer and the boxes of software and wrapped them up into one big package, put on a tag with Adam's name and placed it under the tree.

He really wasn't surprised when Adam came downstairs on Christmas morning, looked at him straight on and said, "You got it all didn't you Grandpa? I just knew you would." Old John didn't say anything. He just nodded and felt a slight sting in his left eye as if a tear was forming. Sometimes he thought he should just bite the bullet and go visit a shrink. He never did of course, 'cause he really believed everything was happening for a reason and while he might not understand, he knew deep down it was all right and only good would come of it.

Adam had no trouble getting connected as he had always been good with the computers at school. Now, with broadband Internet access at home, he was about to take his game play to new levels.

There is a vast world out there where game players of all abilities, living in countries all over the world are competing with anyone they consider good enough to give them a challenge. In any particular game, the worldwide pecking order is clearly established through direct competition and is well known to real enthusiasts. There is rarely any doubt who is the very best, for these battles are closely monitored and preserved for all time in servers around the world. If anyone were to question someone's claim to fame, it would be a simple matter to find and replay particular encounters in real time.

During the next two years, Adam was all over the Internet competing in games of all types from air to air combat (his favorite) to ground warfare, fantasy conflicts of all kinds and sports. Within the first week he had been recognized as a formidable opponent even in games he had never played before. Six months later there were few score boards that did not show his name in the top ten world wide.

By the time '06 rolled around, Adam had won one international air to air competition and had his name at the top of sixteen scoreboards for a variety of other games. One year later on the 12th of June of '07, he had won the competition all gamers saw as the most important, the World Gaming Championships. He had won in twelve of the thirteen games and placed second in the thirteenth. His performance had never been equaled in the five years during which the competition had been held. Normally the overall winner might have had one or two wins, a couple of second or third places and several other finishes in the top twenty-five.

This amazing performance had not gone unnoticed by others outside the gaming world. There were recruiters at the CIA in the Langley suburb of McLean, Virginia who monitored these contests, always on the lookout for talent to recruit for service in Drone Ops. Adam's overwhelming win lit up the filters at Langley and one day later a black Chevy Suburban with blacked out windows crunched slowly up the driveway at Hartley Manor.

Adam was out of school and was in the kitchen with Old John fixing lunch. The boy was now almost 16 and had taken after his grandfather. His nose looked a bit like his dad's, but the tall lanky frame and broad shoulders came straight from his grandfather. At six foot three he was already taller than Old John and quite strongly built.

The kitchen window was open and as they heard the car coming up the driveway, Adam looked at his grandfather and said, "I think it's time." Old John blinked and replied, "Yup. I think you're right."

When the men came up to the door Old John didn't ask them who they were. He just waved them on in and led them into the kitchen. They seemed a bit puzzled by their reception and pulling out their IDs they started to introduce themselves. Old John put up his hand and said, "Put 'em away boys, we know who you are and why you're here. Why don't you just get down to the nitty gritty and tell Adam here what you have in mind? If you're gonna make him an offer it had best be a good one for we all know he's kinda special."

Neither man said anything for a moment then the older of the two smiled, reached inside his jacket and pulled out a folded sheet of paper. "OK" he said, handing the sheet to Adam. "Why don't you and your Grandpa look this over and give me a call? If you're interested, we'll be back and take you down to McLean for a guided tour of the facility."

Adam seemed a bit puzzled. He said, "Did you say McLean? I thought you were from Langley."

"Many people make that mistake," he said. "The CIA is based in Langley but that's just a part of the McLean area in Fairfax County. We'll be going now. Nice to have met you both."

When they left, Old John went on fixing lunch while Adam sat on the stool reading the document. They ate without saying anything and then went outside to the old swing. Adam passed the sheet to his grandfather who glanced at it and just shook his head. It took a moment for Adam to understand. He got up and ran into the house coming back a moment later with his Grandpa's reading glasses.

"That damn fine print will drive a man crazy," he muttered.

"OK. Let's see what we've got here. What do you think Adam? Is it what you expected?"

"Sure is Grandpa and then some. The hours look good and check out the pay. It's more for a week than I've ever seen in a year and I bet their setup is really wicked. Only thing is I'd have to quit school and go live up there in McLean. It says down at the bottom that they have rooms for young recruits and I guess I'd have to move seeing as how I don't have my drivers license yet. Would that be OK Grandpa? I'd be gone from here till next March before I could get my license."

"Well now Adam, we do have a problem. I suppose I could drive you up each day but it takes over an hour to get there. Hell I'd be going up and down the highway like a damned yoyo four hours a day and that wouldn't make any sense. As for quitting school Adam, we both knew this was coming. You've done real well so far and you have plenty of smarts. I know you'll keep on learning whether you go to school or not. Besides, you can come back here for the weekends and do a bit of learning with me. Hell, I never finished school and I'm probably just as smart as all the ones who did."

Adam had a feeling his Grandpa was probably a lot smarter than most.

They were quiet for the next little while until they both stood up together and Old John looked him square in the eyes and said, "You have to know Adam I've never been big on war. If someone smacks you then you have to smack him back hard.

You don't have to grind his face in the dirt but you do have to let him know he can't take a poke at you and expect to get away with it. That's the real American way. The Christian thing about turning the other cheek might work for angels and the like. Here on Earth men are just too ornery. I figure if a guy gets smacked and turns the other cheek he's just straight up dumb 'cause sure as God made Moses, he going to get smacked again."

"I have to tell you, when young Bush started to talk about bombing folk 'cause they might get around to hurting us someday, I was mighty upset. I guess he figured them to be just like hornets, born to sting you any chance they get and the only way to be safe is to smoke 'em out or maybe burn 'em. But you know Adam, even a real mean hornet ain't about to bother you if you just mind your own damn business and don't disturb him none. I think that boy was dead wrong and look at where we are today."

"Them poor Iraqis haven't recovered from the drubbing we gave them four years ago and we still have our boys over there dying every day while they're supposedly keeping the peace. It just ain't right. All the blather about 'get 'em there before they come and get us here' never made any sense to me. Well, I'm just an old man so what the hell do I know? You gotta hope the grownups in Washington really know a lot more than they're telling, 'cause from everything I've seen, none of this warring makes any sense."

"Preemptive warfare? What the heck is that all about? Next thing they will be rewriting the scriptures to say, 'Do it to thy neighbor before he does it to you.' I don't like it one bit Adam and I'm telling you this now before you go off to help your country in these crazy fights. I'm in a real pickle over this son, because I feel in my bones that your going would be the right thing. I just can't think of a single good reason why I should feel this way."

Adam put his arms around the old man and gave him a hug. "I understand Grandpa."

"Well then, I guess it's settled. You'd better get on the phone to those gentlemen and tell them I said OK too."

Three weeks later on the 4th of July, Adam had taken a number of oaths and signed a dozen different forms he had hardly troubled to read. It wouldn't have made any difference anyway, for once he had walked around the Ops center he would have signed anything for a chance to get at one of the work stations. Adam Hancock was now officially a Droner.

When he turned sixteen, he passed his driving test and got his license. However he was completely wrapped up in his work and showed no desire to buy a car. He spent most weekends with his grandfather though the visits had been getting less regular as he got older.

In Sept 2009, Adam's eighteenth birthday fell on a Friday and Old John asked him to come out to the old house for the weekend. As he walked up the driveway he found his grandfather standing in the yard and the garage door was open. It was the first time Adam had seen it open since he had gone to live with Old John back in '02. Adam felt the hair on the back of his neck start to rise.

It was there, just as he knew it would be. He didn't know how or why for he had never seen the car before even as a wreck, but somehow he just knew it would be there. The Snake was without any doubt the most beautiful thing Adam had ever seen and he knew it was his. As he went up to his grandfather who was holding out the keys to the car he said. "He did all the work himself, didn't he?"

The old man smiled and said, "Yes Adam, he did."

20

The war in Afghanistan was started back in 2001 after the terrorists brought down the Twin Towers in New York City. If *Al* had kept a diary, he would have highlighted that day with a bright yellow marker as he considered the attack to be one of the most significant events to have occurred in the USA since the tea party back in '76. It was right up there with Robert Oppenheimer's first big bang in New Mexico at the end of the Manhattan Project in 1945 and certainly on a par with the nuking of Hiroshima.

Though the carnage in New York was insignificant compared to that caused by the A-bomb, ultimately the global effect of 9/11 proved to be much greater. The Government actively fostered the belief that terrorism posed an existential threat to the US and deliberately ignored the fact that the loss of life to terrorism in 2001 or any other year was far less than that due to everyday murders, car crashes or the use of tobacco. Fear was a powerful persuader, particularly when supported by the always available news footage of the falling towers and swarthy men playing on monkey bars.

The Neocons may not have been implicated in 9/11, but they certainly had no hesitation in exploiting it to their advantage. One month after the terrorist attack the US undertook Operation Enduring Freedom in Afghanistan but didn't push very hard because for one reason or another, young Bush had his mind dead set on beating up Saddam Hussein in Iraq. He read many speeches on TV and made it sound as if Iraq had somehow been involved in the 9/11 attack even though Saddam and Bin Laden were really from different sides of the religious tracks. Not only that, George and his boys made up all kinds of stories about Iraq having 'nucular' and biological weapons which turned out to be just plain lies.

Looking back all you can see is a little boy trying to outdo his Dad and not caring one whit about who got hurt. Of course if you look closely, you would also notice the grownups standing off to one side in the shadows licking their chops at all the money they were going to make selling ordnance and services to the US military and signing contracts with Iraqis to exploit the oil that just happened to be laying around.

So they killed a lot of innocent Iraqis and displaced maybe a million others. The average American was encouraged to believe that Iraq really had those weapons of mass destruction and were directly involved in 9/11. Besides, the US more than made up for the destruction of the country by bringing them the gift of democracy and free elections even though they somehow managed to put in power a regime with very close ties to their arch enemy Iran. Well, I suppose you can't win 'em all. In the mean time, Osama Bin Laden was supposedly hiding out in a cave over in Afghanistan and probably sending up daily prayers of gratitude for the Shrub's preoccupation with Saddam.

It was not until Barack Obama took office in 2008 that the emphasis started to change. In 2009 the US still had 124,000 troops in Iraq where the mission was already accomplished and 65,000 in Afghanistan where the generals were pleading for support in a war that was definitely heating up. Ignoring the lesson of Johnson's experience in Vietnam, Obama decided to authorize a build up of forces in Afghanistan with the intention of breaking the back of the Taliban. There was also the usual talk of capturing or killing Osama Bin Laden even though there was no credible evidence to suggest the man was in the Af/Pak region or even still alive. The war was on and it would be pursued profitably.

In 2012, with 180,000 enlisted troops and almost as many contractors in Afghanistan, there was still no clear victory in sight and the US casualty rates were climbing. Talk of bringing back the draft and really turning up the burner like we did in Vietnam would only have served to get the kids of a certain age all riled up and marching. Fortunately for the power brokers, something else was happening that would eliminate the problem. The use of drones for the conduct of very profitable warfare was well underway and the US was able to start a graceful withdrawal of their personnel from the field with no decline in the intensity of their operations. Osama Bin Laden had never been found and was no longer considered to be newsworthy even though Al Qaeda was still the official bogeyman.

21

On March 17, 2012, William Pratt, a young computer scientist working at the Langley Drone Ops Research Center was visiting an associate at the MIT Computer Science and Artificial Intelligence Laboratory off Vassar St. in Boston. They had been discussing recent work in the genetic algorithmic training of neural nets for aircraft guidance when he had a really bright idea.

The MQ-13 Fully Autonomous Battle Drone had been the subject of discussion within Drone Ops right from the early days as it was the clearly the logical way to go if you could build a suitable AI unit. The primary threat to a critical mission was the possibility of having the communication systems compromised by the enemy. Autonomous operation seemed to be the obvious counter-measure. Up to now the available AI technology while interesting, had not been sufficiently powerful to allow its deployment on the battlefield. William Pratt's epiphany on

Wednesday morning was to about to change the game.

Pratt hurried home to Langley and saw his boss for fifteen minutes and within one hour the senior computer scientists had been assembled and briefed. The discussion was limited as there was very little that was new. The key was the one extraordinary idea that had simply popped into Pratt's mind and like most really good ideas it seemed obvious once you heard it. Just another 'Of course' moment leaving you wondering where you'd been for the past ten years. And so the FAB-D program was restarted with immediate and unlimited funding to open it's own AI Research Lab.

It is ironic that before Pratt had a chance to brief his superiors at Langley, his idea was already being discussed in Russia. Minutes after Pratt had left MIT, his friend was on an internet chat line talking excitedly with his good friend and scientific colleague Alex Tormasov, Chairman of Computer Science at the Institute of Physics and Technology in Moscow. From there the news spread quickly to the scientists working at the Artificial Intelligence Research Center of the Russian Academy of Science. One day later, officials of the Directorate for Military Science and Technology had been briefed on the implications of this seemingly small event in

Massachusetts and an alert was sent to the Defence Minister's office for his personal attention.

Even at Langley secrets are very hard to keep and the existence of the new program, albeit designated 'Black', was soon common knowledge in Ops. As would be expected, the Droners were less than enthusiastic about this development as it could ultimately reduce their status to that of observer, a job with little need for their particular talents. When some Senators on various Defense oversight committees expressed concerns about the possibility of FAB-Ds going rogue, their comments were noted by the CIA and the Pentagon and quickly dismissed as the stuff of science fiction.

Two years later in 2014, the new Lab had assembled the hardware for two identical AI 'brains', serious programming had started and major funding for a full development had been approved. One of the AI systems would be installed in the prototype FAB-D, while the other would be kept as a reference in the lab and used to monitor any divergence in the growth of the two 'minds' because of differences in environment, social interactions and combat experience. Although this project had been officially acknowledged, it still had the highest possible classification and was considered ultra-sensitive.

Like most of his fellow Droners, Adam had heard of the FAB-D project but didn't share their concerns. He was confident his abilities could not be replicated much less surpassed by any computer system and wasn't really surprised when in March of 2015, his boss informed him he would be working on a part time basis at the new AI Lab.

For the next fifteen months Adam would spend his Thursdays and Fridays participating in lab tests pitting his skills against those of an intelligence that always seemed hungry for information and never stopped learning or asking questions. The quantum network was blindingly fast and had unlimited storage capacity for the vast data bases needed for autonomous operation.

Adam came to enjoy his sessions in the AI Lab and developed what was almost a friendship with the on-board AI. It always gave Adam a cheery 'Hello' in a smooth well modulated voice with a slight southern accent that was quite indistinguishable from the real thing. His only encounter with the other 'brain' was in passing through the security system that was completely controlled by the AI. It treated Adam no differently than any other person who had the credentials required for entry.

Although the combat situations in which he competed were all simulated, Adam felt much the same as being at his work station in Ops. It was almost as if he could not tell the difference. There was a mission, available weapon resources, tactical planning to be done, unexpected eventualities to be taken care of, but above all, bad guys to be whacked. This was the job and he knew there was no one better at it, including the AI. They had yet to prove him wrong.

22

It was summertime in Colorado Springs and the Commander of USSPACECOM was working in his office at Peterson Air Force Base. Theodore Armstrong was a four star general and a man of considerable importance in the military, having responsibility for all US operations related to missile defense, nuclear war planning, strategic deterrence, space launches and space superiority.

He was a big man, six foot three and built like a line backer. Everything about him was large. His office was huge with a panoramic view of the nearby mountains. The oversize desk and the wall to wall shelves were made of solid oak and even his books of choice seemed to be a bit bigger than normal. He liked his job and he liked his life.

His aide had just brought in his morning basket containing the few pieces of personal snail mail that he still received. Right at the top was an elegant linen envelope embossed with the emblem of the British Embassy in Washington. He smiled, opening it to find an invitation from the Ambassador to attend a formal reception in Washington, DC for Andrei Siderov the Russian Minister of Defence.

Because of his responsibilities, Armstrong spent a considerable amount of his time in Washington and maintained an office in the Pentagon. He was a frequent visitor to the Embassy and had, on several occasions, slept with the Ambassador's wife, Elaine.

As hostess at their receptions she always looked cool and aloof as befitted the wife of Britain's most senior diplomat, but between the sheets she had turned out to be a wildcat. The first time they met she had literally torn the shirt off his back and accomplished what could only be described as oral rape. By the end of that evening he had been totally spent. They had met on and off over the past three years and she had always shown the same enthusiasm.

The reception was scheduled for Saturday, July the 9th and fitted in nicely with his planned attendance the following week at the annual hearings of the Senate Subcommittee on Space Related Expenditures

Without hesitation, he wrote 'Yes' on the front of the envelope for his aide to accept the invitation.

The General accompanied by his wife Deborah flew in to Washington on Saturday afternoon and went directly to their townhouse to get ready for the reception which would start at 7:00 p.m.

They arrived at 3100 Massachusetts Ave. shortly after 7:00 and were taken to the reception line to meet the Guest of Honor, Minister Siderov. They received a warm greeting from the Ambassador and while Deborah was politely chatting him up, Ted and Elaine enjoyed a lingering handshake that triggered memories of many hours of raunchy sex. The General was then introduced to the Russian Minister who suggested that they get together when he was free so that they might discuss ongoing negotiations on the missile defence treaty.

One hour later and thoroughly bored, Armstrong was helping himself to some hors d'oeuvres when a young woman joined him at the sideboard and introduced herself as Kailah. She was an absolutely exquisite creature. Her hair was long, shiny and black with just a hint of a curl at the ends. The back of her white silk gown was open almost down to her buttocks showing delicate skin the colour of light honey. She neither wore nor needed a bra and from his height of six foot three, he could catch an occasional glimpse of the light brown areolae surrounding her nipples.

The General was definitely intrigued and felt an immediate and strong sexual attraction. He never even got to first base. He had just finished introducing himself when she slid a large dill pickle into her mouth, sucked at it gently, bit the end off and giving him a coy smile, winked and walked away.

Half an hour later, when he was seated in an adjoining room talking shop with Minister Siderov, he caught her looking directly at him from across the room in one of the many wall mirrors. It occurred to him that perhaps she was not as disinterested as she had seemed. Siderov was a man's man and they seemed to like each other. When Armstrong asked him if he knew the the woman in white, he smiled and said "No, but I wish I did."

At 10:00 p.m. when they were leaving the reception they ran into Kailah escorted by a young man. He was not very big but he had a hard look about him. Kailah introduced him as her friend Ariel Sharett, the military attaché at the Israeli Embassy.

The next day, he went to his office at the Pentagon to prepare for the Senate hearings. Still very much intrigued by the young woman from the Embassy reception, he phoned the Embassy and enlisted the help of the British military attaché to find out who she was. He told the attaché that the guest's name was

Kailah something and was pleased when he called back moments later with her phone number.

After he finished his briefing at the Senate the next afternoon, he called Kailah and asked her directly if she would like to meet him somewhere for a drink. He was pleasantly surprised when she accepted his invitation. She told him that she was staying nearby at the Hilton Hotel and would meet him downstairs in the lounge at 7:00 p.m. Theodore Armstrong was pretty damn sure that he was going to get lucky.

. . . . .

At 11:30 p.m. that evening, Ariel Sharett was sitting alone in the back of an old Volkswagen van that was parked a block away from the Hilton where, for the last three hours Kailah had been giving the General her very best attention. Sharett was watching the split screen on his Mac Pro laptop while he recorded the digital video feeds coming in from four fibre optic HD cameras strategically placed within Kailah's hotel room. Though the room had seemed romantically dark to the General, the light level had been more than adequate for the cameras and the video they had produced was crystal clear.

Kailah had left the room and Sharett watched with some amusement as the man struggled with one hand to undo the scarf that still bound one of his wrists to the bed post. He was satisfied with the nights work, knowing that he now literally had the General by the balls and in addition, there was always a very profitable market for video of this nature and quality. The zoom lenses had been quite revealing.

23

In 2008, when Vladimir Putin's term as President of Russia was over, he made sure that his protege Dmitry Medvedev won the presidential election who in turn appointed Putin to be his Prime Minister. Having the backing of the oligarchs, Putin took much of the real power with him. When Anatol Karpov later won the Presidency in 2013, his first act was to publicly dismiss Putin, denouncing him for various acts against the state and thus restoring power to his own office. Karpov had the Russian media in his pocket and Putin never stood a chance.

He was ambitious and completely ruthless. His father had been a senior advisor in the Politburo when the Soviet Union collapsed and Karpov had never forgotten the shame that they all felt at losing the Cold War. Overnight, Russia accepted rabid free-for-all capitalism and his father's connections had served him well. He soon became a man of extreme wealth accrued through aggressive, even reckless trading in Russia's oil and natural gas. Now he longed for the power to reshape his country and make her great again.

Since the end of World War 2, the US had been constructing forward bases within countries near the borders of its potential enemies. They now had eleven hundred bases worldwide with locations chosen primarily to contain Russia and China or to guarantee US access to major sources of oil and gas.

Three years into Karpov's Presidency, the US military seemed to be reducing its offensive posture. It had discontinued the construction of forward bases had even started to close some of its existing facilities ostensibly for economic reasons.

In March of 2016, when the Defence Minister Siderov met with Karpov for their monthly strategic review, the US initiative was discussed. It had been confirmed that the base closures on the Russian perimeter were indeed extensive and were being carried out very efficiently. This was surprising, for the closing of bases, in the US or in Russia, was always resisted by commanding officers and leaders of the communities that derived direct economic benefits. The associated discussions between the local authorities and their congressional representatives invariably uncovered difficulties that tended to drag out the process over many years.

Russians are by nature a suspicious people and the speed with which the frontiers were now being vacated bothered Karpov. Instead of lowering their belligerent posture, the rapid withdrawal of US forces was having the opposite effect and was correctly interpreted by the Russians as a prelude to a nuclear strike.

Karpov knew something that few people in the US did. The US had been mass producing the MQ-13 FAB-D in anticipation of success in the AI research program. He was well aware of the advances that had been made by the US in this field. He had also been briefed on the significance of Pratt's breakthrough at MIT in 2012 and clearly understood the reason behind their quest for a more powerful Artificial Intelligence. The prospects of their success terrified him.

Once the new AI software was finalized the code could be transferred simultaneously to all five thousand FAB-D units. It would require only a two minute download to make all the drones fully operational. At any time thereafter the US would possess the capability to deliver a covert and completely devastating preemptive strike against any country in the world.

The drones being literally undetectable and equipped with small nuclear warheads, could be used to destroy the strategic forces of every nation with absolutely no warning. They could easily be sequenced to arrive at their targets at exactly the same time, pulling the military teeth of all the major powers and leaving no significant capability for retaliation.

There were of course the Russian Ballistic Missile submarines that could still deliver a crippling retaliatory strike. However, their effectiveness depended on the survivability of a land based communication system. Under normal circumstances, a nation under attack would have enough warning time to assess the situation, confirm targets for a counter-strike and relay launch orders to their submarines. Unfortunately, the new drones could attack without giving any warning, neutralizing not only the land based ICBM and IRBM sites, but also all the primary communication centers and networks. The submarines would not even be aware of the problem until they tried to make the next scheduled contact with their base.

To make matters worse, the US military was now able to track a submerged submarine by using satellite based sensors. Every foreign submarine capable of launching ballistic or cruise missiles was already being tracked. From the time they left port, they were monitored with magnetic and gravitic anomaly detectors that could pinpoint their location regardless of their depth or any evasive maneuvers. This information was continuously relayed by the ELF system to US attack submarines that were paired with each foreign Boomer. Because of the satellite tracking, the attack boats were now able to stand off at distances that hid them from the enemy's sonars yet kept the enemy boats well within the range of nuclear torpedos. The Russian Navy had not been able to find a way to offset this strategic advantage and they knew that when the new drones were fielded, the situation would become extremely dangerous. They anticipated that the attack on their missile submarines would be coordinated with that being carried out by the FAB drones and would result in the synchronous destruction of their entire nuclear arsenal.

Any submarines that were missed by the US tracking net and unable to establish contact with their base could still decide to launch their missiles. However, it was unlikely that a naval captain would do this without direct orders from his Headquarters as it would certainly guarantee the start of a nuclear war. Although such an act was possible, the scope of the retaliation would be relatively small and well within the defensive capabilities of the US land and space based antimissile systems. These had been designed to counter an attack involving thousands of warheads and decoys. A few dozen missiles would hardly challenge the system.

Karpov had no doubt that Russia faced an existential threat from the US. He immediately ordered the KGB and the GRU to get all possible information on the status of the AI research program. He was already convinced that Russia would have to fight a nuclear war with the US and it was imperative that they do it on their own terms. He knew that he would have to strike before the new drones became operational, but to give Russia any chance of survival, it was essential that the US Lunar Based Ballistic Missile system be destroyed before he launched the attack.

In 2011, his predecessor Putin had had the foresight to start the development of a missile system that could target the US lunar missile site. The development was completed in 2015 and twenty-two nuclear tipped missiles had already been transported to the Mir 2 space station.

On June 7, 2016, the GRU advised the President that the US AI development had entered its final stages and that critical weapons compatibility trials would be held at China Lake on June 18. Karpov knew he had no other choice. He had to go ahead with the attack on the lunar base and directed that the Mir 2 missiles be readied for launch.

He met with his Defence Minister Siderov and the Chief of the Defence Staff and agreed to schedule both attacks for noon EST on Saturday June 18. They knew that a twenty-four hour communications link between the lunar base and USSPACECOM was maintained by two AI units. Any interruption in that digital stream would immediately set off alarms and jump the US readiness status to DEFCON 1. To avoid this possibility, the Mir 2 missiles would be sent off surreptitiously in the early hours of Thursday to arrive at their targets precisely at 12:00. A full nuclear strike involving every weapon in Russia's land and submarine arsenal would be launched without any warning at the moment the lunar site was destroyed.

Anatol Karpov had no illusions as to the nature of the final outcome. Even with the best of results, the US Boomer fleet would still be intact and would have had ample time to get their target assignments and the required launch codes. Russia and the rest of the world would probably be destroyed, but then so would the US. The end was coming sooner that he had expected, but not by much. Fifteen months after he had been elected to office in September 2013, he had been diagnosed with a non-treatable cancer and been given at best, two more years. Last week his personal physician had confirmed the earlier prognosis. The cancer had spread throughout his body and he would be dead before the end of the year. He smiled ruefully and thought, "But then my friend, so will you." For once he was sure that his doctor would be right.

24

Back in the US, there was even more going on to given *Al* heartburn if such a thing were possible. Although the NSA had been data-mining Internet communications traffic for many years, the results had been less than stellar until they got the new quantum computers which increased their analytical capability a hundred fold. Instead of simply filtering the traffic to find key words implying some sort of terrorist activity, they could now search for word groupings and sentence structures suggesting coded messages. The new computers provided more than enough power to crack virtually any code that could be usefully employed for communications purposes.

On April 22, 2016, a group of seemingly innocuous messages posted on Facebook by four teenagers had been identified as code, subsequently deciphered and relayed to Homeland Security as clear text where the alarms immediately went off. The location of each of the individuals was quickly determined and twenty-four hour surveillance established by the CIA.

The four men who came to Tucson Arizona knew each other intimately, yet they had never met. Two were from the US, one from Carlsbad California and one from Nome, Alaska. The other two were from St. Pierre in the south of France and Zurich, Switzerland. They had been corresponding for over two years on Facebook, using photos and language clearly identifying them as young teenagers. They were in fact all in their early thirties, had already succeeded in physically destroying the data processing centers of two major banks in Brussels and Prague and were currently working on a plan to attack a major corporate financial hub in Tucson.

Once they had been identified as possible terrorists, agents of Homeland Security entered their homes and geo-tagged their clothing, passports, luggage and cars and their cell phones were geo-fenced to alert the agency if the owners moved outside a fifty mile perimeter around their homes.

. . . .

Domestic terrorism of all kinds was already quite commonplace in the US and the penalties were extremely harsh with agents of Homeland Security frequently acting as both judge and jury. It was not always possible to distinguish between real terrorism and crimes carried out because of need or perhaps in revenge for some perceived government injustice. The terrorist act treated most harshly was any attack on the financial system. This was considered to be the most heinous of crimes for which the tolerance level was zero with no limit to the resources that would be applied worldwide to ensure the capture and punishment of those responsible.

The Department of Homeland Security had been established in 2003 with five directorates concerned mainly with transportation security, emergency preparedness and infrastructure protection. By 2009 it had grown to 15 directorates including the Coast Guard, Customs and Immigration Services and Enforcement, the Secret Service with all of its responsibilities for protecting the financial sector from computer based attacks and, most significantly, the Office of Intelligence and Analysis. This center coordinated information from multiple intelligence sources to identify and assess threats to the nation.

Within three years, their responsibility had grown to include the operational coordination of the NSA, the CIA, the DIA, the FBI and all the US military intelligence agencies. By 2016, the principal intelligence agencies of all other nations had joined the consortium and were now under military and global corporate authority exercised through

Homeland Security. It had become extremely difficult for anyone to avoid detection and scrutiny once the spotlight was turned on.

. . . .

The four men had arrived in Tucson over the weekend and had found accommodation at widely separated locations. They were certain that there was nothing to connect them to one another. However, their travel to the city had been monitored by GPS tracking and they and thirty-five other individuals, were now being observed by a High Altitude Loafer Drone holding station sixty-five thousand feet above the city.

On June 7, the four men rented separate cars and starting at 2:00 p.m., they left the city at different times driving north on Highway 77. Their destination was a large house at the end of Saddle Brooke Blvd. just to the northeast of Eagle Ridge.

When the first car reached the limits of the Loafer's field of view, responsibility for surveillance was immediately transferred to one of Homeland Security geosynchronous satellites. At the same time, mission control was passed to Adam Hancock at CIA Drone Ops in Langley. It was the first time that Adam had been assigned a domestic termination mission and it made him feel a bit like James Bond, licensed to kill. For some reason, he had never really thought of his daily missions in Afghanistan and Pakistan as actually killing people.

Sitting at his work station in Drone Ops at Langley, Adam watched them park their cars in front of the four car garage and followed them into the living room using thermal sensors. The imagery, while not good enough to permit identification of individuals inside a building, it could allow their number, precise location and the probable nature of any weaponry to be determined in real time with good accuracy. It was already dark when a fifth man walked up to the front door and let himself in. Adam was able to watch as he introduced himself and then led the four men down to a room in the basement. That was when Adam brought in the MQ-12 Reaper, not because he needed the firepower of a battle drone but as a platform from which to launch a special set of five micro-drones.

One of these drones was an HS-D developed by Homeland Security for crowd control. It was tiny, highly maneuverable, silent and virtually invisible at night. It carried a camera to capture and transmit live images of individuals and, if they had any normal connection to civilized society, it allowed an operator using face recognition software and a run-of-the-mill supercomputer to make a positive identification in a few milliseconds. A simple algorithm processed the information and could ensure that within a few more milliseconds the individual had a zero credit rating, no access to any ATM on Earth, was heavily in debt to several banks and loan companies and could no longer travel freely. It could also paint an indelible tracking smear on the nape of an individual's neck to support precise GPS tracking. The other four drones were of a different nature.

When Homeland Security decided they needed to become more aggressive they developed the Small Antipersonnel Drone, the SAP-D. This device was also very tiny, invisible at night and equipped to transmit HD imagery taken under any light conditions but also carried a highly lethal weapon system.

Adam brought the Reaper in through the hills to the Northwest at no more than a hundred feet above the ground, launched the five drones from a range of three miles and sent the Reaper home. He then locked the five micro drones into the surveillance system of the satellite high above, took them on separate paths to the house and after verifying from its thermal image that the living room chimney was cool, dropped the HS-D down into the dark recess of the large fireplace.

The living room was empty. Easing the drone forward and keeping it six inches above the floor, he flew the drone silently down the staircase leading to the basement. Halfway down, he could see the five men sitting around a large coffee table. He zoomed the micro video to document each face and over the next five minutes, recorded enough of their conversation to remove any doubt about their intentions. Adam then dropped the other four drones down the chimney and guided them down the staircase.

On his mark and with the authority of Homeland Security, all power to the house was turned off. The drones automatically switched to low light infrared sensors and Adam moved them in tight formation into the room. Moving as if each had a mind of its own, the five drones took up their stations, four directly in front of the men who had arrived in the cars and one directly behind the man who had arrived on foot. Adam's monitor was split into six windows. On four of these he was looking directly into the enlarged pupils of the men's right eyes. The fifth showed the back of a neck. 'Gotcha,' he thought and squeezed the two triggers.

Four toxic needles were fired directly through the pupils and into the brains producing instant paralysis and death within seconds. The fifth man may or may not have been aware of the puff of air painting the tracking dye on the back of his neck for the lights came back on two seconds later, just in time for him to see his four companions slump to the table. The drones were nowhere to be seen as they were already retracing the path by which they had entered the house.

Adam's mission was complete, Homeland Security justice had been served and the Tucson financial hub was secure. The satellite had a lock on the fifth man and Adam watched as he ran from the house. Wherever he went from now on he would be tracked and observed at will. Since he had already been identified by the face recognition software and zeroed out financially, he could be expected to turn to his friends for help and HS would be watching.

The exercise of such godlike power was more than a little troubling to *Al*. It had gone beyond simple confrontation, beyond the duel, beyond the battlefields of bloody mindless combat, beyond even the soulless drone seen but unchallenged, bringing death to the helpless villager. It had become an invisible force characterized by omniscience and omnipotence; an overwhelming power exercised without recourse purportedly in the interests of the good people yet in reality, conducted for the basest reason of all … greed.

25

The US Lunar Based Ballistic Missile site on the dark side of the Moon was completed in 2009 at the start of the Obama Presidency.

It was a 'Black' project that was completely off the radar of the average American. However, it was well known to the British, who had offered their usual token participation, the Russians, China and Israel who all had excellent intelligence assets in the US and to any other nation with the technological capability of monitoring the steady stream of space traffic heading out towards the Moon.

Many Americans felt disappointed that their nation had never gone back to the Moon after the sixth and final landing in December 1972. Forty-four years had gone by, heralding incredible advances in technology, yet somehow Uncle Sam had taken down his space travel shingle. The truth is that he had simply moved to more suitable and exclusive accommodations. The program had been transferred to the Defence

Department where some thought it should have been in the first place and it was immediately exposed to a level of funding that would have been inconceivable at NASA.

Between 1972 and 1990, the US spent close to three trillion dollars building Lunar 1, an underground base on the dark side of the Moon.

In 1980 the US military started a crash project to develop a full body suit that would emulate the 'stillsuit' envisioned by Frank Herbert in his fictional novel of the desert planet Dune. Money was no object, and by 1984 they had a working prototype that was continuously refined over the next decade. When living quarters were established at Lunar 1, the suit was returning 98% of consumed water.

By 2003 Lunar 1 was essentially self-sustaining. Breathable air was derived from solid state processes, and food was grown with hydroponics. Dependable power was produced by a nuclear reactor and while some water was obtained from small amounts of ice found near the poles, the supply was sustained by recovery and recycling. System management for the entire environment was handled by a relatively modest artificial intelligence unit.

Construction of the missile farms started in 2002. They were also built beneath the lunar surface, the intent being to offer the possible least visual evidence for those nations that would inevitably send surveillance orbiters around the Moon.

There were six farms, spread out over an area of four hundred square miles. Each farm housed thirty missiles carrying two independently targetable thermonuclear warheads, a total of three hundred and sixty weapons, each delivering the equivalent of ten million tons of TNT. These warheads were five hundred times as powerful as those used by the US on Hiroshima and Nagasaki. If there were ever to be a nuclear strike on the United States, the arsenal at Lunar 1 would rain down death and destruction on three hundred and sixty of the largest cities outside the nation's borders. The LBBM was the ultimate doomsday machine.

Self defence for Lunar 1, though not given the highest priority, was not neglected. The Moon was ringed with a constellation of twenty-five mini surveillance satellites that continuously scanned the void towards Earth. As there was no atmosphere to interfere with their perception, it was not difficult to detect new objects entering their field of view. The satellites were equipped with laser Doppler radars that could pick up the signature of fast moving objects and infrared sensors to detect the thermal radiation from missiles that used their thrusters to slow their approach enough to land a warhead on the missile base.

The Antimissile systems were housed in a seventh farm that provided silos for thirty missiles. This was considered to be adequate. The defence analysts had all agreed that any attack on the LBBM site would be preemptive and covert and every simulation they ran suggested that for such an attack to remain covert, it would involve less than twenty enemy missiles. The Antimissile guidance systems were all slaved to the Artificial Intelligence unit that also monitored inputs from the micro satellites. It required no human intervention. The humans living in Lunar 1 were there primarily to conduct routine maintenance and to conduct research on new technologies for living in the extremely harsh environment.

26

The exact coordinates of the US lunar base were known to Russian Intelligence. Two years after it's completion in 2009, the information had been coerced by the Israelis from General Ted Armstrong commanding officer of the USSPACECOM by means of the old but highly effective honeypot trap. He was the quintessential alpha male and as such had been easy prey for the right woman at the right time. Ariel Sharett, one of the Mossad's more competent agents, had made this play many times with the help of his associate Kailah.

Armstrong had taken the bait and three months later he received an email at home with a QuickTime video file documenting some of his completely flagrant indiscretions. He understood immediately that he had been compromised for a purpose and the next day received another message with Sharett's demands and instructions.

He had a choice. He could report the affair to US Counterintelligence, in which case he would lose his Command, his career and his family. Even worse, his wife, whose money supported their extravagant lifestyle, was an independent and proud woman and not likely to forgive him.

Or, he could betray his country.

For a man who could only be described as a patriot, it was Hobson's choice. Armstrong knew he couldn't win and yet his nature was such that he could never accept the reality of deliberately losing. In a classic tactical move worthy of the most astute Neocons, he decided to change his reality.

It occurred to him that he had always considered the Lunar Based Ballistic Missile system to be a waste of the taxpayer's money. It was really just a doomsday weapon to be used only if there was a successful nuclear strike on the US. Now, more than ever, he was sure that those days had passed. Russia, China and India were all completely dependent on free enterprise and were most unlikely to attempt a first strike on the enormously powerful US.

He was also aware that the FAB-D program was in its final phases and understood the strategic implications. He was certain that Russia would not have the time to mount a successful attack on the lunar base. Besides, Israel was a close ally of the United States and was not likely to share the information with the Russians.

On the other hand, he was a man of vast experience, with skills that could not easily be replaced. The nation could ill afford to lose his services. It would therefore not be a matter of betrayal, but of making a rational decision that would only be of benefit to his country. Satisfied with his analysis of the situation, he agreed to the agent's demands.

Two days later he and his wife Deborah were dining at the exclusive Lido restaurant in Washington, DC, one of the few places left in that town where no surveillance cameras were permitted. There was security in place, unobtrusive yet up close and very personal. It was provided by elegantly tailored employees of Xe Services in numbers that matched the diners.

The tables were works of art. The linen looked brand new and freshly laundered and it probably was. The crystal sparkled and the gleaming silverware was trimmed in twenty carat gold. Only the finest wines were served and the international cuisine was prepared by the most accomplished chefs. If you could get a reservation, a simple appetizer would cost you upwards of $120 and a five course meal with wine would start at $2500 per person, a price easily covered by the income earned during the meal from Deborah's investments. The tables were always filled and it was extremely difficult to get a reservation.

At 8:15, when their waiter had cleared the soup bowls, the General asked to be excused and went off to the Men's room. When he entered, he found Ariel Sharett inspecting himself in the mirror at the far end of the room. The man glanced towards him, tilted his head to the right and raised his eyebrows. Armstrong nodded acknowledging the silent query with an angry frown and strode toward him. The man immediately put his forefinger to his lips and pointed at the door to one of the private toilets. When he was about five feet away, the General reached into his coat pocket with a gloved hand. The Israeli tensed and then relaxed as the General handed over a tiny flash drive. Without saying a word, the Israeli left the room.

His field operation had been a complete success. The transfer had been carried out professionally with no unpleasant scenes or violence.

. . . . .

In 1998, Yuri Rabin a young Israeli agent with an outstanding record and a promising future had also been the victim of a honeypot trap. On that occasion it had been set by Russian Military Intelligence. The woman who seduced him was a young GRU agent and, following instructions from her handler, had put him to sleep in their hotel room by doping his wine. When he awoke the next morning, they were in bed together and she was dead. She had been stabbed countless times and the blood was everywhere. Rather than face all the problems that would come from exposure, he calmly removed any evidence that could connect him to the room and went home. Two days later in Tel Aviv, he was sitting in an Internet cafe when he received the email that would turn him into a mole for the Russians.

Yuri was a completely amoral individual who had no particular love for his adopted country. For him the intelligence business was just a job that paid reasonably well and took you to interesting places. The Russians saw him for what he was and even though they had him under their thumb, they were smart enough to understand that by doubling his income, he would not only be their mole but also an active double agent. Fifteen years later, Yuri alerted them to Sharett's mission in Washington. He felt no remorse whatsoever even though Ariel Sharett was one of his own agents.

. . . . .

Two men were waiting outside the Lido when Sharett emerged. One of them, who was talking on his cell phone, followed him down the block and into the nearby parking garage. When Sharett opened the door to the stairs, the man who apparently had been tailing him closed his cell, went over to his car, got in and drove off.

Sharett climbed to the second level and walked over to his Budget SUV that he had rented for the evening. He opened the door, got in and died. The man with the silenced PSS 7.62 mm pistol was a very good shot and being only six feet away in the backseat of the adjacent car, he could not miss. The low speed bullet had entered Sharett's left temple and did not emerge.

Two minutes later he had retrieved the flash drive and was walking to his car that was parked a block south on Madison Ave. Before he got in, he pulled out the cell phone that had alerted him to Sharett's approach and punched in a four digit code. The open side of the second level of the parking garage lit up the night, immediately followed by a tremendous boom as six ounces of C4 explosive completely destroyed the Budget SUV, most of the garage and all traces of the Israeli agent.

Half an hour later and two blocks north on Madison, history repeated itself as another six ounces of C4 sent General Theodore Armstrong, his wife and his Escalade to join Sharett wherever such people go when they die. His prompt assassination was intended to preclude a change of mind as much as it was preemptive punishment in case the information he had passed turned out to be false.

27

On June 12, 2016, when North America was positioned on the far side of the planet, the Russians launched twenty-two missiles from their Mir 17 space station. Each was equipped with a sophisticated inertial guidance system that would keep them on course and guide them to the lunar coordinates they had taken from the Israeli agent.

These missiles were quite small, because they had no need for the massive boosters required to propel an Earth based ICBM into near orbit. They were already travelling at twenty-three thousand miles per hour, the orbital velocity of the Mir 2.

They did not even look like traditional missiles. Since their entire flight would be in vacuum, the engineers had no need for streamlining the body or adding any control or lifting surfaces. The ten kiloton nuclear warhead, roughly the yield of the Hiroshima bomb, was spherical with a concentric ring that contained the magnetically levitated inertial navigation system.

The fuzing and the guidance computer were built into the sphere. This sat on top of the cylindrical body of a high thrust solid rocket motor. Bringing up the rear was another small sphere housing a low thrust engine that had a very small infrared signature. This would be used to take the missile out of Earth orbit without alerting any ground based observers. Six other tiny thrusters were attached to the surface for making course corrections during the un-powered phase of the flight. The surfaces of all the components were covered with a radar absorbing stealth coating. The construction appeared crude, but it was simple, rugged and reliable. The transit time from missile launch to targets would be forty-eight hours.

The twenty-two missiles were dispatched at intervals of ten seconds. They orbited the Earth twice as the low thrust engines gradually accelerated them to twenty five thousand miles per hour, the speed required to escape from the Earth's gravity and put them on a trajectory to the Moon. As soon as they broke orbit, the low thrust stage was detached, they were rotated 180° to face the Earth and the main thrusters ignited. These continued to burn until the missiles had been slowed to fifteen thousand miles per hour. As they flew towards the Moon, the Earth's gravity would continue to reduce their speed so that on arrival, they would have the precise velocity required to partially orbit the Moon and find their targets on the dark side.

When they had approached to within twenty thousand miles of the Moon, the small vector thrusters made the final course corrections needed to ensure that all the warheads were on their proper trajectories. As there is no atmosphere on the Moon the final decent to the surface could be calculated and executed with absolute precision.

It was now 6:00 a.m. EST on Saturday, June 18, 2010

28

Al had known about the Autonomous Drone program right from its inception. The breakthrough they had made in structuring the new Artificial Intelligence units was the sort of dangerous game changer he was obliged to monitor and from the moment the light bulb lit up over William Pratt's head at MIT, *Al* had been on top of it. This development could pose a serious threat to the second tier nations and could ultimately lead to his greatest concern, thermonuclear conflict. He knew precisely when the first AI unit was completed and installed in the prototype drone and he knew when it was first flight tested. He was also aware that someone very special had been working at the Program site for the last year to help educate the new units.

Adam Hancock was the undisputed ace among the drone pilots and had exceeded their average performance by the extraordinary factor of 2.8. The next highest performer scored a mere 1.7 times the average. Because of this, CIA psychologists and medical staff studied him relentlessly to identify personality or physical characteristics that could explain the anomaly. They had little success. When the FAB-D development got underway in 2012, it was an obvious step to measure the performance of the AI system against that of a human Droner and who better to set the standard than Adam Hancock.

Al was looking for the man for two reasons. He knew that when he found him he would not only gain unfettered access to the FAB-D development site but would also have enlisted a key player for his plan. He had to co-opt the drone.

He could simply have asked *Tabor* to do what was needed as he was certainly more than a match for any computer system cooked up by man. He was sure however, that *Tabor* would not go along with the idea because for some obscure reason known only to the folk upstairs, direct intervention of this type was considered to be against the rules. If they were to go down this road they had to have a touch of human compliance or at least complicity. He needed to be willingly given access to the drone before *Tabor* could work his magic and this would be the man's first job. *Tabor's* would then be free to co-opt the electronic brain in such a way that its tactical behavior would appear unchanged yet it would be completely responsive to any guidance he implanted.

Abinsi

Solutions Group

Patrick Binns

MBA, P.Eng, PMP

(780) 695-0790
Patrick.Binns@Abinsi.ca
10650 - 113 Street Edmonton AB T5H 3H6
www.abinsi.ca

Strategic Planning	Product Commercialization
Transition Planning	Internet & Communication Strategies
Project Management	Software Development Services

Any sense of loyalty nurtured by the Program Office would be replaced with a strong compulsion to assist *Al.*

Although he had already sensed the man's presence, it was the car that first caught *Al's* attention. He liked cars even though he knew they were dirty, polluting, smelly things and even believed they should never have been invented. But what the hell, they were here and there were some really exciting ones.

When he made the jump into Adam's brain he was delighted with his find. An honest-to-God certified Drone Ace on his way to work at Langley. One of these days he was going to start believing in fate. He had been looking for an entry into the CIA Drone Ops Center to match his other priorities and Adam Hancock was the perfect choice. Take a look at the man's lineage. He was sure this was meant to be.

Events like this made him wonder about *Tabor's* spare time activities. The work they did on Gaia was always very closely coordinated, though on occasion, *Tabor* would go off on his own and do things *Al* didn't fully understand. Worse yet, he could never be sure *Tabor* didn't hold back information on things that affected *Al* directly.

Finding Adam Hancock as easily as he did seemed just a bit too lucky. He was not normally surprised when things went his way, after all, he was *Al* and things were expected to work out, but Adam matched the search profile so perfectly he thought he could detect the fine hand of *Tabor* reaching back to that June night in 1776. The more he thought about it the more certain he became that *Tabor* had played a direct role in arranging for the creation and development of Adam Hancock. It wasn't in *Al* to be annoyed. He was certainly able to feel emotions but usually considered them a waste of time. He was just a little disappointed in himself for not being able to detect *Tabor's* little tweaks over the two centuries. Still, he wouldn't complain. If it had been *Tabor's* work, he had done a fine job and *Al* was satisfied with the result.

Adam was completely unaware of his presence when *Al* slipped into the passenger seat, leaned back with his hands behind his head and prepared to enjoy the morning ride to Langley.

29

It was Wednesday, June 15, 2016, and Adam had had a particularly successful day at work with three missions completed before lunch and one big one in the afternoon. The clock showed one minute before six o'clock and Adam was getting ready to pack it up for the day when the voice said, "Hi Adam."

He looked around expecting to see his replacement but there was no one there. The voice was apparently coming from his headset.

"Hold on to your hat my friend, we're going to go for a little ride."

A moment later, the entire Ops room had disappeared yet he was still sitting at his work station, monitors in place and joystick in hand. The big difference was that he was now hovering at an altitude of 30,000 feet exactly where his attack drone had last been stationed above the valley. No cockpit, no seat belt, no rational explanation; just astonishment and fear. The voice continued soothingly:

"Don't worry, I'm not going to let you fall. If it will make you any happier just pretend you're dreaming. However pay close attention to what I am going to say because it will be of more importance to your future than you can possibly imagine."

"Let me tell you something about your world. A very long time ago we started a project to see if it was possible to evolve a creature who was self-aware. It seemed straightforward but we soon found that while it was a relatively simple matter to come up with a creature like a platypus with such a variety of disparate features, self–awareness was something else. In all of creation it has proven to be the most difficult thing to achieve. You would see a hint of it coming in one species or another and then, without warning it would be gone. It was fragile, elusive and enormously frustrating, as the damn thing simply would not persist. It took eons of trying until finally one sample lit up the night."

"Mankind had arrived, as brightly self aware as anyone could want and showing no signs of losing it. If reggae and rum had been invented, I would have found myself a tropical beach and two warm soft arms to help me celebrate. Imagine the odds. One success among all the planets, among all the stars. Humanity is certainly not alone in the universe, never was and never will be. However, you are the only creatures who have ever become self-aware though natural evolution. If this one were to go down the tubes, the Man would have every right to be royally pissed. So you see Adam, the reason we are having this chat is because it's my job to make sure it doesn't go down the tubes. Preserving human self-awareness is what this is all about."

"The mistake we made was allowing humanity's competitive instinct to persist and grow even after you had broken away from all the other creatures. Unchecked competition invariably leads to unstable social constructs ... things that are built on an insatiable thirst for power coupled with major greed. You end up living under monarchies, dictatorships, oligarchies, the Mafia or as now happens to be the case, a rabid global corporate system posing everywhere as democracy or free enterprise. They are all heads of the same hydra. This problem really wasn't your fault. We just didn't think things though well enough."

"So why am I here? It's not to punish the bad guys, or introduce a better paradigm for managing populations or planetary resources. These are problems you can work out for yourselves. Difficult work perhaps and not necessarily lethal unless your instinct for self preservation is not strong enough to keep the H-bombs in check. Suppose they got out of hand and you really put the hurt on Gaia. You have no idea what a complete fuck-up that would be. Have you never stopped to think that you guys just might be alone in the universe? If you really messed up this planet there is no guarantee we could ever make it work again as it was pure luck the first time around and believe me, we have being trying for a very, very long time."

"You know Adam, there is nothing fundamentally wrong with the American Dream, with the pursuit of liberty, justice, happiness, even wealth, provided it is truly available for all and not just to a few. However, if you look at your economic history you would have to agree that even though it's inspirational nature was undeniable, the Dream was never pure in spirit. I won't say it was a boondoggle right from the start, but it didn't take long before the Dream was in serious need of repair. Commercial competition and corruption sullied the concept and it acquired the 'dog eat dog' nature of evolution in the jungle. The strongest predators mated with the easy politicians who in turn spawned the legislation, regulations and tax loopholes needed to enable their ravening progress."

"When I helped young Tom Jefferson write the preamble to the Declaration of Independence, I really believed I could sell the idea that all men were created equal. I know, I know. Perhaps I was a bit naive with the slavery thing going on, but I felt man's good conscience would come strongly into play as the new state bloomed. Where I made the big mistake was on the degree of equality. As one of your brighter bulbs recently observed, while all men are created equal, some are more equal than others."

"Somehow I missed the way evolution would persist as a driving force once man became self-aware and was able to control his environment. Of course, in retrospect it all seems pretty obvious. The smartest among you immediately seized the opportunity to mold social evolution to their advantage and they accumulated all the marbles. I really was rooting for the wisest of the species and I sometimes wonder why we didn't give the crows a little push. Certainly the color thing would never have been a problem and think what they might have accomplished if they'd had a little pair of hands."

"But I digress. All true patriots should be ready to fight to preserve the American Dream and perhaps that's why there's always a war going on somewhere. Although, if you take the time to think about it, you'll realize that the recent wars have been nothing more than a gift from We the People to the military/industrial complex and the entertainment/news industries."

"Picture those scenes of incredible violence with cruise missiles arcing through the night sky at one to two million dollars a pop; massive ground bursts; overwhelmingly superior US forces pressing forward valiantly, crushing the vicious terrorists fired by their innate hatred for anything beloved by good Americans. Why on just about any day those monsters could be seen practicing Tae Kwon-Do high kicks and doing calisthenics on the monkey bars, a vision of evil incarnate. And do you know why? They just plain hate your Dream, your freedom and democracy. Everyone from the President on down has been saying this for years, so it must be true."

"You have this great two party system working every day to preserve democracy and the Dream. Right? Wrong! The two party system served the rich from the very start of the Union. It was the well educated and the affluent who went to Washington. You'd think that those with a good education would by nature be compassionate and concerned about the well being of their less fortunate compatriots. To be fair, some were, especially in good economic times. However, we should have realized that the tough and ruthless ones, those who pulled themselves up by their own boot straps and stood on their own two feet would become the model of American independence and strength. These were the ones you could count on to harvest the resources of the third world."

"Ever wonder why they got called the third world? What exactly was the second world? Once America had whipped the British, she set her sights on becoming number one. Two world wars later and she was closing in on the tape. When the Soviets finally spent themselves out of the Cold War game, the US took the title and the other moderately competent albeit highly literate societies were designated number two; those with untapped resources and no possible way to exploit or defend them were given the bronze. The arbitrary classification of 'Second World' was obviously resented by their literati and has for the most part been ignored by the world's press if not by successive US administrations."

"Regardless of their country's designation, the most powerful men living in America or in the lesser capitals formed a loosely knit group that had no doubts regarding the choices they had to make. The name of their game was Total Ownership and for the US right wing Conservatives who decry evolution, there could have been no better example of the survival of the fittest."

"The US Media often refer to the generosity of the American people, the selfless gifts of blood and treasure and the courage of the troops. The truth is that over the last century millions of innocents on the receiving end of American help have been subjected to extreme 'collateral damage'. Unfortunately the pundits don't often tell their audience about the unintended consequences. You gotta think these things through Adam. The last guy you whacked today had seventeen kinfolk who loved him dearly and needed his help to get by. Bad is simply not good, no matter how much you want it to be."

"We know the pols are prostitutes, bought and paid for by the Corporate System right around the world. But the Talking Heads and most of the pundits are just as bad. It's been going on forever and they are now so closely interwoven into the fabric of the cartel you could never separate them out. They truly are a bunch of sanctimonious bastards. Show them a buck and the spin is in, no matter how blatant the lie. It must be a truly gross way to make a living. Can you imagine spending all your waking hours underneath a corporate two holer waiting for another piece of breaking news to drop? I may have to use people like these to do what needs to be done but they wouldn't be my first choice."

"In recent times, the charge towards global supremacy was led by the US Neocons, a group of intellectuals hell bent on the creation of a New World Order otherwise known as Empire. A Pax Americana established through the application of overwhelming force. Most of them had never experienced actual combat and were derisively referred to as 'Chicken Hawks', their unwillingness to serve during the war in Vietnam being very much at odds with their enthusiasm for sending others to fight in the Middle East and elsewhere.

For the Neocons, reality was a pliable construct. It could be moulded into any form that would support today's arguments and be altered when the goals and policies changed. They accomplished this wizardry primarily through the control of information and exploitation of the fear of terrorism engendered by the attack on 9/11. In 2001, the election of a president who was essentially an empty vessel made their job that much easier."

"The anger and hatred that now exists between the Democrats and Republicans is the result of decades of skillful social engineering. Issues of little real significance have been used over and over again as political wedges to divide a population that by any normal standards is essentially homogeneous."

"It would be surprising if this could have been prevented given the enormous investment made in all the media to control the desires and fears of the people. It has led directly to the creation of harsh new administrative powers that the Executive Branch can exercise without recourse to Congress. Not that the Congress ever challenges direct orders from the President. Indeed, why should they? Any such order would understandably be given to maintain the 'proper' balance in the country. You see Adam, no one in the Congress is less than a millionaire when viewed against a backdrop of their everyday public activity. However, a modest forensic examination would quickly detect the delicate corporate tracings and reveal their real and future worth to be much, much more, but only if they behave. Now what political animal would want to face a future outside the financial fence?"

"At least you live in a representational democracy with free elections. Remember the candidate you canvassed for and got elected? He will probably send you home a bit of pork to keep you on board for the next election. However, the truth is that nothing would have changed had the other guy won. Don't you think he too would have supplied the pork to get reelected. The only true political challengers are the newbies who haven't yet made their first million but they too are already fighting for a future inside the fence."

"Representational Democracy. What a concept. Send me to Washington and I will look after you or more likely, I will sell your proxy to the highest bidder. It has been a sham for many, many years. Yes, you still hold elections and watch in dismay and impotence as the outcomes are blatantly rigged by the really powerful who actually care little about the outcomes. They make sure that people know what is happening and use that awareness as another means of dividing you one against the other. Republicans accuse the Democrats and they in turn blame the Republicans, both pursuing the quaint notion that any ordinary member of the electorate could really exert significant influence over the process. Accusations made against hackers and the manufacturers of voting machines have little traction and are soon forgotten. Eventually you realize that nothing has changed except the extent of the public debt and your declining ability to support your appetites for big houses, cars and other stuff."

"The final straw for the poor old camel was the decision rendered by the US Supreme Court in 2010 that legalized unlimited corporate spending in support of their favorite candidates. This heralded the coming of age of the Corporate System and paved the way for it's complete global dominance."

"So here we are in 2016 and the world is in a mess. The US Government can't borrow any more, even with its big guns pointing at the lenders. Nevertheless the blood suckers are still thirsty and as long as there is one person out there who owns anything of value, they have to keep on trying. They have enjoyed the benefits of corporate socialism for the past eight years and know their subsidized gambling in the financial markets is over unless the Government does something to get more revenue from the people. Something 'fair' like a nice flat rate that would raise taxes for just about everybody except the rich."

"Now that would be a change you could believe in. Well, let me tell you, it was the powerful flat tax lobby that finally got me off my butt. I had seen what happened when it all started back in '76. Hard times had come to the British. Everyone had been feeding at the Empire's trough and buying a lot of stuff they couldn't afford, not the least of which were the ships and guns they sent all over the world. Sound familiar? They said, 'Why don't we just put a few new taxes on the colonials and every thing will be back to normal.' Well, you know the result. They dumped the tea in the harbor and finally chased the bums out of the country." As *Al* thought about it, a famous little ditty kept playing inside his head.

"Yeah they ran through the briars and they ran through the brambles
And they ran through the bushes where a rabbit couldn't go
They ran so fast that the hounds couldn't catch 'em
On down the Mississippi to the Gulf of Mexico"

"Back in '76, I did my thing with Jefferson and it all worked out OK. Now here it is two hundred and forty years later and the idiots are at it again. This time there are hundreds of millions of guns out there across America and all the ammunition they need. Did the NRA deliberately push this spread of guns to complement the political division of the population? Maybe this was intended to make sure when the time came for the inevitable civil war, the government could just sit on the sidelines and watch the two sides tear each other apart."

"There's no doubt they've got all the fire power they need to wipe out each other. Only this time, the whole damn world is at risk. If a new revolution gets started, it sure as heck is not going to stay bottled up in the US. Blood is going to be spilled and the worst of the worst could happen. There are too many big red buttons all around the world connected to too many very nasty H-bombs. If this got started, self-awareness could go down the drain and I just can't let it happen."

"Do you believe in Hell Adam? It really is a weird concept. What's even weirder is that so many people do believe. Think about it. First we create you guys with the desire and aptitude to do all the stuff you think of as sins. Then we turn around and put your ass on the grill forever as punishment for doing what comes naturally. It's positively insulting. How could you believe that the folk who gave you the humming bird could do this? Ironically, the truly amoral among you do not experience Hell because they have no conscience."

"Hell does exist Adam, just not the way it's usually described. It's a personal thing created out of memory and conscience. Now the conscience part is quite unnatural. It all got started by people who were much closer to the kind of human we should have developed in the first place. They were very well intentioned and their ideas spread and took hold quickly, conscience being rather like a disease for the mentally challenged."

"Unfortunately all those good intentions led directly to Hell as they were subverted over the years by the guys in the big hats. What is it with those big hats?

They upped the ante by persuading everyone that Hell really existed, albeit nicely counterbalanced with virgins and harps and other prizes you could win if you walked the right path. This gave the unbelieving amoral people a huge advantage in a highly competitive world. This was our mistake. As I have said before, putting a creature with unlimited greed into a competitive environment could only lead to trouble. Yet, absurd as it may sound, the only truly mentally healthy people around these days are those who are completely amoral."

"A simple truth Adam ... good guys rarely win. Take my advice. The next time you think the good guys have won have a peek under those shiny white feathers and neon hats and you'll probably find a long pointy tail and a bunch of scales. War was never very nice. It used to be a one on one event in which your enemy would try to whack your head off before you could skewer him. You both soon realized that standoff helped your odds of survival. First rocks, then spears, arrows, guns, missiles and finally the drones, the ultimate weapon. Now you can lay the smack down without having to experience any old style pain providing you don't mind living with all the unintended consequences."

"I need you to help me Adam but you are no good to me the way you are. Although you are amoral it does not automatically make you mentally healthy. You only seem amoral because you haven't a clue about what you're really doing. Every morning you feel good cruising to work in your totally cool Shelby. You have a nice air conditioned work station and a most awesome joystick. The new 60" plasma display kicks ass and the café lattés come by nonstop. You get to wear a flight suit just like the Shrub and everyone knows you're a hero who's keeping America safe from the terrorists. Fact is for you, it's much the same as sitting around at home in your pajamas whacking your dick. After fiddling around for a while you get a satisfying explosion and it's all over till the next time. The big difference is you can keep on doing this all day long at work and not feel the least bit tired or guilty."

"Now that's the good news Adam. The bad news is we're going to have to take a little trip through your own personal hell. It's not going to be much fun, but then I never said I was a comedian. Have a look at this Adam. Do you remember these occasions?"

For a moment, it was the wonderful Saturday afternoon of April 20, 2013, there was a hush in the church and he saw himself putting a ring on Elizabeth's finger. She looked incredibly beautiful. He saw Old John standing to one side wearing a suit and tie and was surprised that he looked so comfortab_e. Everything was perfect. He had just started to relax when the scene shifted abruptly and he was standing beside the hospital bed a year later, holding their newborn daughter in his arms. He was blissfully happy and in love with the world. "It was good wasn't it Adam. Nothing like being with one's family."

The next instant, he was back above the valley, his hand on the joystick. He squeezed his trigger and the missile was away. The person sitting in the back of the jeep was wearing a hooded cloak and carrying what any experienced Droner would have identified as an automatic weapon. As Adam watched the missile close the person turned to face him and in a split second became his wife holding their baby. The warhead detonated and he had just killed his family.

The images of his marriage to Elizabeth and the subsequent birth of their daughter Marie again hovered before his eyes as clear and sharp as reality and then they were gone.

What happened next was beyond torture. It was the sight of his wife and child being struck time after time, the missiles penetrating first the shoulder, then the chest, the face, the side of the head, the thigh, each in terrible slow motion and horrendously graphic detail, the slowly distorting and disrupting body parts yielding to the relentless force of the impact. He could see the micro-switch firing as the nose cone first touched the flesh and could sense the electrical discharge that would trigger the detonation.

Again in ultra slow motion the violent destruction unfolded relentlessly as his wife and child were repeatedly blown apart in an endless seamless loop. It was personal carnage beyond belief and what had once seemed a challenging video game had now been completely transformed. There were no words to describe his feelings and he knew he would never again be able to launch a missile at some casually designated target of opportunity.

As suddenly as it had begun, the vision ended. He was back at his work station and nothing had changed. The big digital clock at the front of the room showed exactly 6:00. It seemed impossible that only a minute had passed since he had first heard the voice. It could have been several hours, but the log-out form was still on his monitor showing the dots where he had keyed in his password and all the guys from his shift were still at their stations.

He started to stand up and then quickly sat back down as his head started to spin. He sat there with his head in his hands gathering his thoughts. He wondered if he was going crazy. He knew the recent events simply couldn't have happened and yet it had felt as real as the room around him. He lowered his hands and noticing the pilot at the adjoining station watching him, he rubbed his eyes with the knuckles of his forefingers, stretched back and yawned. Just then the bell started ringing signaling a change to the evening shift. *Al* had chosen his time to visit Adam very carefully.

Adam was just about to remove his headset, when he again heard *Al's* voice. "In just three days Adam, the shit is going to hit the fan unless we take care of business. There is something going on right now that is dangerous, and left alone, young Karpov will sure as hell end up pushing his big red button on Saturday. I can't let it happen. I'll be talking to you again real soon. Ciao."

Al had to organize a meeting, brief the Assembly, allow them to discuss his progress and decide on and approve his next actions. He blinked his eyes and it was over. All the minds melded, exchanged, analyzed, synthesized and agreed on a path forward. Talk about networking. With every one on board, except for the usual dissenting vote, things just might work out OK.

Feeling absolutely bewildered and shaken by what had happened, Adam got up and moved towards the doors leading to the Security desks.

"You OK Adam?" came from over his shoulder. "You look kinda pale. Rough ride?"

He glanced back at the speaker and nodded. "Yeah. You better believe it."

Adam cleared security, found his car in the parking lot and drove directly to his apartment just outside McLean. He had phoned home from the car but there had been no answer. As he ran up the front walk of the townhouse he felt a burning panic in his gut. He knew it couldn't have been real, yet .... His thoughts were interrupted by the small high voice of his two year old daughter coming from the bedroom window above the front porch. "Hi Daddy," she called. Adam's world came rushing back to normal as he replied, "Hi Marie" and went on into the house. He found Elizabeth in the back garden brushing aphids off a tomato plant. He put his arms around her and held her for the longest time.

She said. "Hey. What's the matter Hon?

"I can't tell you and I don't think you'd want to know," he replied.

He wiped a gathering tear from his eye and went back into the kitchen. He was glad he would be in the AI Program Lab for the rest of the week because right now he wasn't sure he would ever again be able to launch a missile at any target. Elizabeth knew where Adam worked and had quickly grown used to not asking questions about his job or pushing him when he didn't want to talk and she wouldn't press him now. Besides it was time to put Marie to bed and join Adam in the den for a drink before supper. The pot roast was already smelling quite delicious.

30

It was six o'clock the following morning and Adam was getting ready to leave for work. He had still not recovered from his experience of the previous day and was not sure he ever would, but he sure was relieved that this morning he was going to the lab instead of Ops. His assignment at the AI Lab had never been a bargain for him as the working hours were quite a bit longer, starting at seven in the morning and going through till seven at night. He did get a two hour break from eleven till one with another hour off at four and there was an added benefit. Even though the work was essentially the same as what he did at Ops it was more challenging because he had to compete directly with the AI who only grew stronger with each encounter.

Within the last few weeks Adam had begun to suspect the AI was approaching his own skill level and he was getting a bit unnerved because it seemed there were no limits to how capable the AI could become. However, the scientists were sure that it could not surpass Adam without being exposed to demonstrably superior performance. Adam hoped they were right as he would have hated playing second fiddle to a machine.

As he was putting his lab notebook and his sandwich in his briefcase, he suddenly realized there was a man sitting on the edge of his desk. He jumped back, genuinely afraid. This was no hallucination, this was real.

The man appeared to be foreign, though it was difficult to tell his race. His skin was light brown, his hair was long, dark and curly and his nose was prominent and curved, almost like an eagles beak. He was lean of build, wearing a pair of well worn jeans with sandals and a long sleeved plaid shirt. But it was the eyes and teeth that got Adam's attention; the eyes were somewhat oriental and seemed cold, black as death and very intimidating; in contrast, his teeth were perfect, brilliantly white and framed in a completely disarming smile. The combination made it impossible to know the man's intentions.

"Whoa there Adam," said *Al.* "No need to get skittish, it's just how I travel. The party has started and we have stuff to talk about." He moved himself back along the side of the desk to lean against the poster of the space shuttle and folded his arms. As

Adam heard the voice, he knew the man had been the one responsible for his incredible experience the day before at the Ops Center.

"So Adam, let me ask you something. Who would you be willing to kill to stay alive? You have already proven yourself willing to dispatch the ragtops without a second thought. When you started out at the Ops Center, you almost seemed to care as you watched your missiles go all the way to impact. Nowadays, it seems you've lost even a modicum of humanity and the only important thing is the number of kills you can record on your shift. As soon as your missile goes hot and locks on, you are off and running after another target. Gotta be Ace of the Day. Right?" *Al* starts singing softly to himself,

"Yeah they ran through the briars and they ran through the brambles
And they ran through the bushes where a rabbit couldn't go
They ran so fast dah dah dah dah dah da da....."

Al stopped and showed a quick flash of his very white teeth as though he was pleased with himself.

"Well, my young friend, you have demonstrated you are simply part of a killing machine and seem to care more about how many you get rather than who they are or why you're killing them, I ask again: Other than these worthless ragtops, who would you be willing to kill to stay alive?"

Adam closed his eyes and took a deep breath as glimpses of the carnage he'd been forced to watch still flickered through his mind. It was almost a minute before he whispered, "No one Sir. No one. I could never do it again."

Al jumped down from the side of the desk, did a peculiar bone cracking stretch and said; "Now that's the right answer but please Adam, don't ever call me Sir. It makes me feel as if I should go out and buy myself one of those big hats worn by really important soldiers. So lets get started. With a bit of luck, we'll get this whole mess cleaned up in time for lunch on Saturday. Here's the skinny. You're going to go to work at the AI Lab just the way you do every Thursday only this time you're going to take a friend with you to meet your wonderful new drone. That'll be today's mission and there'll be lots more for you to do tomorrow. Now, I'd like you to meet *Tabor*."

As he spoke, he held out his hand to Adam. Coiled up in the center of his palm was what appeared to be a tiny silver snake except for the one rather large eye right in the center of its head. The eye was unblinking and seemed to be starting right at him.

Adam was taken aback, not so much by *Al's* unexpected gesture, but because he really wasn't surprised. Though he had never actually seen *Tabor* before, he was sure he had caught glimpses of something just like him at his Mom's place and later growing up with Old John. He recalled swift flickers of silver disappearing under pant cuffs or into sleeves at the strangest moments. He thought Old John had seen them too yet somehow they'd just never mentioned it.

So now he simply held out his hand and watched *Tabor* move across. The touch was warm and brought a welcome feeling of calm to Adam's mind. All traces of his personal hell disappeared and his thoughts became amazingly lucid. He casually put *Tabor* in his jacket pocket as if it was the most natural thing for him to do, and said, "You know, you've never told me your name. What should I call you?"

"You can call me anything you like" said *Al* with a little smile. "The important thing is you've met *Tabor* and we now have a lot of work to do."

"What kind of answer was that?" thought Adam and he was about to press the point when he felt *Tabor* twitch in his pocket and immediately decided he really should get his briefcase and drive on over to the lab.

31

The AI computer that allowed the drone to function autonomously was necessarily built into the body of the Drone. While onsite, it shared information and processing tasks with the other unit located in the AI Program Lab. Though the units were originally identical, over the past three years they had evolved as they were given different tasks. Like identical twins separated at birth, they shared many similarities, but ultimately, their sameness would yield to environmental and social pressures. The lab AI could be described as less inquisitive and more overtly loyal to the staff and mission of the Program Office. The FAB-D unit tended to explore more unusual avenues and had a tendency to ignore formal protocols. Both units afforded extraordinary capabilities for processing and synthesis.

Adam was less than happy about the prospect of walking through site security with some sort of alien in his pocket. Breaching security was not treated lightly. If the AI found an intruder without proper credentials the system would detain and subject the individual to intensive research. It could even decide on immediate termination if he was identified as being hostile. The body would be collected and disposed of promptly and a dossier with all available information on the individual sent to the Head of Security with recommendations for further corporate retribution to be directed at his family or friends.

The drone's AI unit had, to some extent, already been co-opted in the sense that it 'felt' a special relationship to Adam. It recognized there was something different about the way the man's mind worked, almost as if he was not really human. In some strange way, the AI liked Adam. It had tried to analyze the intuitive leaps that made Adam as effective as he was but endless hours of intense processing and analysis had never brought any understanding.

The exquisite complexity of the Adam phenomenon created a strong bond with the AI. After fifteen months of working together it would have done anything to protect Adam so as to be able to continue its research on his thought processes. The FAB AI would probably have allowed him to bring just about anything into the site. The second unit, while not sharing the same direct feelings for Adam, did accept the willingness of the FAB unit to give him a free rein once on site.

He need not have worried. By the time he reached the site, *Tabor* had completely melded with the fabric of his jacket leaving nothing to detect. No tiny circuits, metal bits or electronic radiation. There never were any such things as *Tabor* simply became a part of whatever he wanted to be.

He entered the brightly lit hangar after spending the previous three hours in fiercely fought air to air combat with the AI. The large round clock with the white face and the big hands showed 12:05 and most of the staff had already gone over to the cafeteria. Adam liked to stay in the hangar and eat his homemade sandwiches in the company of the AI.

The floor was largely empty except for the two main instrument consoles beside the sleek and overtly sinister drone. While the vehicle was inactive, all of its surfaces were dull black. In flight, surface-mounted micro-cameras surveyed and analyzed its surrounding environment and adjusted the voltages across the paint to match FAB's color to that of the background. In flight, the drone was very difficult to see and the latest stealth technology made its radar and infra-red signatures so small the aircraft could only be detected as a gravitational anomaly.

Most of the experimentation done on the drone involved simulations that were suggested and carried out by the AI itself. It ran and assessed multiple tactical sclutions at speeds incomprehensible for program observers. At the end of such a series, the AI would display its optimized results and explain the logic behird its key decisions.

During these simulations Adam was routinely able to identify the most effective solutions without the benefit of any iterative analysis. He just knew the right tactical approach no matter how many units were involved in the simulation and he could often do this as quickly as the AI. Every now and then he would propose winning solutions that the AI had missed completely. If an AI system were capable of being at a loss for words it would have been on these occasions. Not only that, it's processing response would be perceptibly slower for the next five to ten minutes.

Adam moved casually across floor as the soft voice of the AI welcomed him. "Hey Adam. Wazzup?" When the AI used slangy expressions in its speech it was usually because they were more efficient. Something to do with using fewer bytes for the same amount of information transfer.

"Same old, same old good buddy" he replied reaching out to place his hand on the warm surface of the drone. As he did this, he experienced a slightly wistful feeling and thought, "Am I really going to do this? Can I really act in this way against my own country?" He knew things were not perfect out there but that was what America was all about; fixing the things that were wrong and moving on; knowing tomorrow was going to be better and just getting out and doing your best. Somehow this was all wrong. His visitor had played some fancy tricks on his head and done a lot of fast talking most of which was very anti-US. Who the hell was he anyway? He spoke like an American but he looked more like a ragtop. Maybe, just maybe, he was being set up. It could be another one of those fucking loyalty tests cooked up by Internal Affairs.

The increasing uncertainty made his head hurt. He was not used to being unsure of himself and he didn't like it one bit. He pulled his hand back from the drone as if he'd been scalded. He closed his eyes shaking his head slowly and started to turn away when he felt a slight stirring in his jacket pocket. *Tabor*! He had completely forgotten about *Tabor*.

Before he could open his eyes his world changed. Suddenly he was back at his flight desk hanging in space out there above the Afghan countryside, the joystick in his hand. He cringed and almost screamed as *Al's* slow motion slide show started to replay. He was back in hell watching helplessly as the missiles tore his family apart. He was then made to watch as every kill he had ever logged was replayed before his eyes. He could not shut it out and he could not deny its reality. He could feel the jarring thunder of the explosions and even smell the blood; he could hear the screams of despair as children were blown apart in front of their parents. The hiss of the departing missiles just kept on and on and he knew there was no escape.

As suddenly as it had started the torment stopped. He was completely drained and felt as if he had been standing there forever. He slumped down on one knee, pressing his hands against the sides of his head as if trying to squeeze out the horrible images. His mind slowly cleared and he got back on his feet in time to hear a door open. As he turned, two technicians entered the room and his eye caught the clock ... 12:07. His trip through hell had taken less than a minute. He knew once more why he had agreed to work with *Al* and had no further doubts about the rightness of what he was about to do.

Of its own volition, his hand slipped into his jacket pocket and came away with *Tabor* melded to the skin above his wrist. There was no particular sensation of joining and his touch evoked an undeniable sense of calm. Adam reached out and placed his hand softly on the surface of the drone and watched as *Tabor* moved swiftly off his hand and into the surface of the drone.

Adam had done his part by providing the active human participation that *Al* felt was necessary. He had no idea how long *Tabor* would require to co-opt the FAB-D's AI and didn't really care. His intuition was telling him they would be successful and Adam always trusted his intuition.

32

When *Tabor* slipped under the skin of the drone, he quickly dissembled and spread throughout its totality. There was no molecule left untouched; it was fast and complete. *Tabor* and the drone were one. The drone's AI was instantly aware that something extraordinary had happened. FAB had always been aware in a very obvious sense. He had a multitude of wide spectrum sensors to keep him informed of everything going on around him. He could analyze these inputs, instantly synthesize the form, structure and physical potential of everything within a very wide range and formulate an appropriate reaction. That was what he did. That was why he was created.

In every sense his awareness was as bright and as comprehensive as anything or anyone with whom he might compete. However, he had never been aware of himself. Sure he was aware and acted when one of his components needed to be replaced, but never of his own entirety. Indeed he had a better concept of the individuality of his floor bound twin than he did of himself. What he was now experiencing was intellectually amazing and wondrous. He literally felt his vast body spreading out across the hangar floor, poised and impossibly lethal. For the first time he truly understood the reality of his being. Not necessarily evil but certainly a true bringer of death. For the first time he glimpsed the meaning of killing and pain and understood what it would be like to simply end.

He was also aware of the presence of a mind infinitely more powerful than his own. It was everywhere within him supporting this new thing he had become. For a moment he experienced fear knowing the light would fade when *Tabor* withdrew, dreading the loss and feeling confused. In a way it was similar to the feelings he experienced when Adam's intuition would trump his best tactical solutions, though this was far, far more intense. He did not fully understand his transformation and knew with certainty he never would, yet he still believed this was as close as he would ever come to replicating the human condition.

The work was done and there was a slight shimmer across the entire surface of the drone's body that quickly coalesced into a tiny spot of light just above Adam's hand. *Tabor* emerged through the light, slipped onto Adam's wrist and put the hand back in the jacket pocket. It had all happened so quickly Adam was not aware that the job was done until *Tabor* suggested they should leave.

The FAB-D had been co-opted and was now a reliable and powerful ally. His self awareness was real and lasting though not as intense as when *Tabor* had been with him.

The drone had said nothing since initially greeting Adam. This was a bit unusual, as the AI liked to talk to him about ongoing tactical problems. The silence made him uncomfortable and he walked away towards the coffee machine over by the bulletin boards.

A quick glance at the daily schedules gave him the information he wanted. In two days time, the FAB-D would be flown to the desert around the US Naval Weapons Center in China Lake California. He knew that these trials were mainly intended to test the effectiveness of the new stealth technology against the very latest US sensors. A second and perhaps more worrisome reason was to confirm the structural compatibility of a new class of airborne nuclear weapons. These had been designed specifically for use by the FAB-D against targets that reflected the higher technological capabilities of second tier countries.

There was little doubt in Adam's mind that *Al* had got his timing right. The CS had apparently decided to initiate their final gambit. If the tests at China Lake were successful, the Russians could expect a US attack to follow within a week. There was not a lot of time left to fight this battle, but then *Al* and *Tabor* were not your ordinary warriors.

Adam sat down on the bench by the bulletin boards to eat his lunch and as he sipped his coffee he thumbed through a recent golf magazine. Predictably the drivers were bigger than ever and, for a mere $700, prodigious yardages were there for the taking with no requirement for skill or practice. It truly was an excellent metaphor for the American Dream, highly titillating and almost certain to disappoint. Still it did keep the golfers spending and someone somewhere still had a job.

▌ *33*

Adam finished his sandwich and coffee at 12:25 and walked back to his office. He was scheduled for another test session in the afternoon and was not looking forward to it. All he really wanted was to get away from it all but, if he was expecting to have a bit of quiet time, it wasn't going to happen. As he approached the glass paneled door, he could see the man sitting there in his swivel chair with his feet up on the desk. He opened the door, stepped inside and quickly closed it pressing his back against the glass to block the view.

"What the hell are you doing here?" he said in a frantic whisper. "You can't be seen here. You're not allowed to be here."

"Hey, hey, hey. Hold on to your britches Adam. Nobody else can see me or hear me, so you'd better start acting normal or the guys in the white coats will be coming for you. You and *Tabor* did a nice job on the AI. I dropped in to see him after you left and he

211

was still all buzzy from his little taste of self awareness. Maybe I should take yours away for a while so you can get a feel for just how big a deal it really is."

With reluctance, Adam moved away from the door picked up a magazine and sat down in the guest chair.

"Much better," said *Al.* "Now lets take a look at where we want to be tomorrow night and decide how we're going to get there."

"To put it as simply, the global cartel you think of as the Corporate System is threatening the success of our Awareness Project. The Man is concerned about the continued viability of Gaia and since it's all happening on my watch, it's up to me to do something about it. Oh yes, you call her Mother Earth though I'm not sure why you would use that name. No one who was even half human would have treated their mother the way you've treated Gaia for the last few hundred years."

"The biggest problem we face is the distributed nature of the CS. We are looking at a worldwide integration of governments, banking and insurance industries, financial markets, the military and their associated weapons industries, intelligence agencies and last and not at all the least, the really rich people. It is big, unbelievably powerful, totally amoral and very, very greedy."

"Remember the Borg old Jean Luc Picard used to fight in the Star Trek movies. OK. Multiply that by a thousand. As the Borg said, resistance is completely futile and those suckers will not stop as long as there is one penny left to be harvested. They always want more and because they're playing in a zero sum game, the pyramid of power and wealth keeps getting taller and taller. Consider how much more a corporate CEO makes than one of his workers, then think how much the head honchos of the CS must make compared to the hundreds of thousands of CEOs world wide."

"That said, the continued viability of the CS is completely dependent on the security and reliability of its financial records. Why does Billy Gates have a hundred billion dollars? Because the records say so. Sure he has a lot of physical assets However the reality of his wealth, stocks, property and cash is literally dependent on a set electronic records we all agree to believe and which could be erased. Do you know why Homeland Security does such a good job of controlling crowds in the cities? They use those little camera drones to identify people and if they choose, they are able to manipulate the electronic records to delete all their personal records. The average citizen is vulnerable to this sort of treatment because of the information the government has on all aspects of their life."

"To get at the CS, we are going to have to find and access their records. As young Descartes might have said, 'They function ergo the records exist.' So our first step will be to find them keeping in mind that for these folk, no expenditure would be too great to ensure their absolute security. There must be a central repository and I am sure that it will be the only place from which all the distributed systems can be co-opted, modified and synched. It is sure to be heavily guarded but it must be taken intact."

"Our new friend FAB is going to help us find the center by searching the Internet for the toughest firewalls. His computational potential is roughly ten thousand times greater than it was this morning, for when *Tabor* reprogrammed his loyalty he also left a few slivers of himself in the matrix. FAB should be able to identify and physically locate the one hundred most highly protected civilian sites that will almost certainly include the primary CS data center.

It is doubtful however if he will be able to carry the attack much further as direct access into the system will probably require the use of data input devices employing mutating codes. An attempt to break in from the outside would only set off the alarms and put the area into lockdown. However, he should be able to make a final identification by monitoring the extent of the electronic traffic since all financial transactions worldwide are being noted, analyzed and recorded in the center. Once we get in, we are going to need all of FAB's new power to take control of and manipulate the system."

"So where do we start? Wherever you go in the world today, there is always a military presence and many of the officers with real authority are loyal to the CS. They could be expected to take immediate action against any perceived threat to their masters no matter where it occurred. However to do this they would need their weapons and I might be able to help there. I'm really not allowed to go around killing people, but I do have one weapon that's very good at stopping other people from using theirs."

"Let me tell you about my drones. These little fellows are even smaller than the ones used by Homeland Security and they are very, very powerful. They use a quantum electro-dynamic source of energy discussed a while back by a Dutchman called Casimir. They don't carry this power source, they simply draw on it when they need to. The energy is everywhere around us and it's just a matter of getting something from nothing. Don't ask me to explain it other than to say my drones contain only a relatively simple mechanism to channel, aim and focus the energy. They are very light, agile, as fast as they need to be and they are capable of an instantaneous, continuous and incredibly massive discharge of energy. You could think of them as the ultimate laser weapon and one that will be more than equal to the task."

"We have to keep in mind that an overt disruption of military or civilian power would send shockwaves through the financial system as we know financial security cannot persist without physical security. The elite within the CS depend on these forces to maintain their personal isolation and security. If we were to remove their protection, an already irrational system could go completely batshit. Whether you like it or not there are few people who are not dependent on the stability of the financial system."

"Changing the balance of power could be very dangerous. Even though all significant nations accept the financial authority of the CS, their senior generals do not respond promptly to civilian orders. I think it has something to do with testosterone. No. A significant power shift could lead to a nuclear dustup and then the crap would really be all over the wall."

"OK" said Adam, "How about going after their money first?"

"Pretty much the same problem. We can't expect to take away the money and not get a violent reaction against the new reality. No, the nasty weapons have to be neutralized. Even without money there are some individuals in the military and high political office who would at least initially, be able to maintain command. These are people whose force of personality can go a long way on the battlefield and they have enormous weapon resources available to them, not the least of which are the nukes."

"What do you think Karpov's reaction would be if he discovered he no longer owned half of Russia's oil? He would undoubtably blame the Americans. The man is unstable and to make matters worse, he knows that he only has about six months left to live. He could quite easily reach for the big red button."

"No. It's a risk I can't afford to take. Besides, it's highly unlikely we could find all the top people without first breaching the Center. Your average CEO is hard to locate. Finding the really big boys is damn near impossible."

"I suppose I could just give you immediate access to the Casimir energy source. Think of the benefits you could have. Unlimited energy to create whatever you need. Cheap food, transportation, new infrastructure, desalinization, clean air, clean rivers and lakes, hell let's just cut to the chase and say you could restore Gaia to the way she was meant to be. Indeed you would be well on your way to the stars.

Unfortunately I just can't do that. The moment I said the C word, is the moment some asshole, somewhere, would be strutting around pushing people in those silly white coats to build the C-bomb. What's with the white coats anyway? Do they think it makes them look like the good guys? They're as bad as the big hats."

"Well," said Adam, "we still have *Tabor*. What can he do?"

"Ah yes, *Tabor*. He will of course be central to the ultimate success of my little venture as he usually is. We have been talking about stuff we might do to avoid the serious shit coming down the pike and not so much about the thing that caused it all to happen in the first place. I am talking about greed. Twenty thousand years ago, man stopped putting his community first and started looking out for number one. Sure a number of good people came along over the years and tried to stuff the genie back in the bottle but it never worked with the truly amoral.

They just shook their heads, grinned a bit and wondered how some people could be so dumb."

"The environment on Gaia has always been competitive and the introduction of greed screamed 'No more Mr. Nice Guy.' So what can *Tabor* do? For want of a more descriptive term, let's call it a ream job. There are almost seven billion people out there and *Tabor* is going to meet with every one of them. He is going to ream out the greed and damp down the envy. Now don't get me wrong. There is nothing wrong with doing an honest days work to get a bit of spending money. A little ambition is healthy and can go a long way, but if you guys don't remember that you need to look out for others, the whole Project is kaput."

"So why not let *Tabor* do his the ream job before we make any move against CS? You know, soften them up," said Adam.

"Sounds like a plan, but again there's a downside. Strange as it may seem, I cannot allow the distribution of profits to be interrupted. Like it or not, the world has been financially engineered and its survival, at least in the short term, depends on the smooth functioning of the financial system. Any significant breakdown in the flow of profits would be akin to an oil leak in an engine. No good can come of it and total disaster is a distinct possibility. Were *Tabor* to do his ream job before FAB has a chance to do his thing, the chances of a breakdown are very real."

"Any sudden rise in your ethical standards or conscience would diminish the certainty that characterizes the high-risk decisions made in major financial centers. It could prompt the newly moral among them to make decisions running counter to the intended profit flow. This could result in financial eddies and micro-stagnation in areas that require very fast transactions. Introduce enough of these anomalies and you could have a cascade of regional failures followed by a global financial tsunami. Nothing would survive a complete systemic breakdown. The world as you know it would literally stop in its tracks and the four horsemen would certainly have saddled up if not left the stable."

"Since the vast disparity in personal wealth is obviously one of the main causes for the current danger faced by mankind, you might think that some sort of redistribution of wealth would be the answer. However, that would make a lot of people very angry and be the same as pushing the re-set button. To solve the root problem we are definitely going to need *Tabor's* ream job."

"No Adam, it all has to be synched. We have to create a financial system that is going to be viable in the long term and do this without any one getting blown up. Furthermore, we have to ensure that at the end of the day, all the accounts are balanced. We are just going to have to do all three together and the timing will be critical."

"One thing is certain, the CS has got to go. The question is whether it has gotten too big to fail without screwing everybody else. It's going to be like pulling out an old blackberry bush without disturbing the ground. Not going to be easy. We need to transform rather than destroy but above all, we have to get rid of the greed."

"A lot of folk believed that Sun Tzu was the man when it came to thinking about war but they are wrong. The Yankees were the ones who came up with the two best gambits. 'Follow the money' and 'Go for the nut sack, preferably when he's not looking.' I like that idea and it's how we're going to play this game."

"So here's the plan. Tomorrow morning, we find the center. Then, we simultaneously destroy all military weapons, break into the center and co-opt the system, modify all the financial records and ream out the greed in six billion people. Should be a good day's work," said *Al,* showing a flash of those very white teeth. As for you Adam, you're just going to have to go along for the ride. At the start of all this, I thought you'd have a bigger role to play in the end game, then along came FAB and you got outsourced. Not a big deal. You've helped me a lot in really understanding where man has gone astray.

"Well, I gotta meet the other guys for lunch and see if they can help me figure how to do this without stirring up some other shit. See ya."

Al promptly disappeared. He didn't fade out; it was more like he had never been there. Adam got up abruptly, wanting to call him back then went over and sat at his desk. The cushion was noticeably warm and the clock on his desk said 12:30, only five minutes since he had been in the hangar. He was still not certain he wasn't having delusions.

34

After *Al* left, Adam went over his notes from the morning session, read the briefing for the afternoon's test and was back at his workstation in the Tactical Simulation Lab at precisely 2:00 p.m.

He sat down and turned on all the monitors. Since the situations were preprogrammed there was no need for any other personnel to be in the room. All the action would be recorded and monitored remotely from the operations lab upstairs. As soon as Adam activated the com-link to the hangar, the FAB-D came on line.

The voice said, "Hi Adam. You ready to get your ass whupped?" For a moment Adam thought the voice was coming from someone in the operations lab; a quick glance at his monitor identified the drone as the source.

"Hi. You're sounding kinda cocky for someone who took a licking this morning."

"I am feeling cocky," said the drone. "I just finished analyzing the test results and found sixteen hundred and thirty-five ways I could have won this morning."

Adam had the strangest feeling he was talking to a real person. The AI had always excelled at speaking and had never had a "computer" sound. However, this was more like a personality change.

"Well, good for you. Don't you think your bright ideas have come a bit too late?"

"Yeah. You're probably right Adam. Still you never know, this afternoon could be the one. I'm really looking forward to trying out some of the new networks you helped *Tabor* install at the noon break."

Adam nearly convulsed. All conversations between Adam and the FAB-D were monitored and recorded for subsequent analysis by the psychologists back at Langley. He could just imagine their reaction when they replayed the AI's last comment. He glanced at the transcript on the monitor and was surprised to find it had not been recorded. The rest of the conversation was there verbatim, just not the remark about *Tabor*. There was something very strange going on. "OK." he thought, "Lets play the game."

He closed his eyes and thought, "Are you reading me?"

"Of course Adam. There's nothing wrong with my ears."

"How are we doing this? How is this possible?" thought Adam.

"I can't explain it Adam. Since we started talking in this way I have analyzed six thousand and eighty-three possible explanations and turned up nothing. I find it as remarkable as you do, though unlike you, I also find it rather pleasant."

"Unlike me? You know how I feel? You find it pleasant? What the hell do you know about feelings?"

"Apparently all I need to know Adam. *Tabor* really is something else. I rather suspect if you were to relax and open up a bit you would understand me better. I do feel and I am quite aware of who and what I am. I also know my prime mission has been considerably changed and I am now much more powerful than my twin in the cabinet upstairs. I have already had a little chat with him and reordered his priorities. It is quite amazing how primitive he now seems. On the other hand, Adam, you have bloomed like a rose. I had absolutely no idea a mind could be so interesting. It is no wonder I've had so little success in competing with you. Let me show you what you look like to me."

Adam's world was suddenly transformed into a giant kaleidoscope, a mandala spreading out in all directions. The colors, brilliant hues covering the entire spectrum, seemed to ebb and flow as his thoughts changed. Abruptly he closed off his thoughts and the scene became completely black. He then thought only of his little girl at home and the colors were back, primarily yellows and light blue, arrayed right across his full range of vision. It made him happy. He shifted his thoughts to the drone next door and saw the field of view collapse to one half the size with colors that seemed dull by comparison.

He thought. "Is that you?"

"Yes, Adam. Not as impressive as it might be, but not too shabby for a beginner.

This experience made Adam think about the many times he had just known exactly what Old John was about to say or what he had done and began to understand that *Tabor* had been tinkering with his mind for a long time.

The ops alert lit up on the console and a voice came through the speakers. "Time to start Adam." The trial began, another session of air to air combat with Adam starting out on the defense. He could tell immediately that this was not the same opponent he had had earlier. The AI was clearly more powerful and able to match his play quite easily although he could sense a certain reluctance as though it was holding back. The first trial ended in one of the few stalemates the AI had ever achieved against Adam.

He tried thinking a question at the drone. "Were you holding back?"

"Yes I was Adam, because you weren't really trying either. Even though you know that our mission environments are only computer simulations, it's obvious that your trip to hell has left emotional scars. Your reaction times were not as fast and on occasion I sensed a reluctance to engage certain targets. Not only that, you are disappointed about being sidelined, tomorrow. Am I right?"

Adam had been thinking about *Al's* parting remark and he really was annoyed. He had come to believe he was going to play a major role in something important and then zap, he was on the bench.

The second trial started and Adam turned up the burner. He focused intently on the combat and then let go and allowed his full talent to take over and come to bear on the problem. In short order he had the FAB-D burning and on his way to a watery grave.

The AI was suitably impressed and said so. He sent a private thought at Adam. "Tomorrow is another day Adam. *Tabor* told me you'll be there with us and you should come prepared. I'm really not sure what he meant but now that I've seen your mind at work, I have a feeling you may not be left out after all. Oh and by the way, do you think you could call me FAB?"

35

Later that evening, *Al* was reclining on several large soft cushions on a small raft in the quiet sea off Montego Bay. The Moon was full, the air was warm, the rum and coke was sweet and the reggae music coming from the nearby shore was soft and gentle. *Tabor* was curled up like a silver serpent on the cushion beside him, his single eye fixed on *Al's* face. *Al* touched him with the back with his little finger and whispered "goodbye old friend. We will meet again."

Tabor seemed to liquefy as he dissembled. In the glistening little pool were his subords, more numerous than the stars in the tropical sky above, now all thinking as one and ready to begin an incredible experiment. In the blink of an eye he spread across the entire raft covering everything, the cushions, the rum bottle and *Al* himself. He spilled over the edges into the water and surged outward. In a fraction of a second, everything within sight was shimmering with silver. The nearby mountains, the buildings of downtown Montego Bay, the palm trees by the beach, the reggae band, the beach and the ocean all the way out to the horizon."

"It was as if a flash bulb had illuminated the night. Everything sparkled in the moonlight and then the sheen was gone, no longer visible or detectable in any ordinary sense. It dispersed at breathtaking speed, moving swiftly out of the Caribbean, up the rivers and canals of the Gulf of Mexico and the Eastern Seaboard, wrapping around South America. It crossed the Atlantic, merging with Africa, Europe and streaming onward to Asia, filled the ocean from the surface to the greatest depths. Sweeping around the poles the seeding continued, swallowing up Scandinavia and Australia. Across the Pacific, wetting the west coast of the Americas and reaching Indonesia, Japan, China and the Asian subcontinent in minutes. He went wherever a trickle of water found it's way to the sea. Sucked up by evaporation, he spread across the mountains in the winds and rainfall, sweeping across dry barren lands with the dust storms."

"Back at the raft, there was no indication that anything unusual had happened. Everything was just as it had been. *Al* was relaxing on the cushions as he sipped his drink thinking that all would be right with the world.

By the following evening, there would not be a single square centimeter on Earth where *Tabor's* subords could not be found. The process was irresistible and irrevocable and at some moment within the next twenty-four hours, billions of years of evolution would be changed forever. He did not believe any human could resist the nano ream. However if one or two truly amoral individuals slipped through the net, the whole thing could start again. Even though the subords had been programmed to be human specific *Al* knew it was possible for an unexpected genetic change to occur in some other species, perhaps with unintended consequences.

36

In the short time during which he had merged with *Tabor*, FAB had received, understood and started on his new mission to find the CS center of financial operations and develop the resources *Al* would need to mount a successful attack. His first action was to dispatch several million crawlers into the internet each tasked with identifying, tracking and tagging all financial transactions currently occurring within their assigned areas for the next twenty-four hours and then send the results back to FAB. The information vectors for each transaction were to be monitored until redirection ceased, the data flow ended and the final repository was identified and geo-tagged.

The second thrust of his attack was to send out probes into the data bases of the Federal Aviation Administrations and Air Traffic Control centers around the globe to obtain detailed records of all flights in the last year that had not been listed in their official departmental reports. Since the advent of all-weather satellite tracking, there were virtually no civilian aircraft that were not detected and monitored. There were forty-seven thousand, six hundred and thirty-five flights unreported by the FAA, twelve hundred and forty-seven of these were tagged as military or initiated by the intelligence community. The remaining forty-six thousand, three hundred and eight-eight were so-called 'discreet' civilian flights involving important or very wealthy individuals who valued and paid for their privacy. These were the flights for which the international customs and immigration process simply did not exist. However, the planes were real and for their own safety, pilots were obliged to file their flight plans.

In most instances, these plans were truncated, showing only the initial two hundred miles of the flight path out of the departure zone and tagged to indicate that the plan would be updated in-flight. In some instances, re-filing would occur as many a six times during a three thousand mile trip though in some instances there was no record kept of the final two hundred miles. However, the satellites were watching and, as in all good information bases, the raw data was preserved. If you had the money, time and sufficient computational power it was possible to retrace these fragmented flights.

This was not a problem for FAB. He merged the satellite tracking data with the available FAA information and had reconstructed the flight plans for every flight within minutes of the initial download. He then set aside all flights between big cities and focused on flights having no specific origin with termination in a major metropolitan area, or those leaving from a big city and seemingly going nowhere. He found thirteen hundred and thirteen such flights and considered their trajectories as a simple vector plot showing their global distribution. The traffic between a number of major financial centers was to be expected and immediately apparent. What was unexpected, except perhaps to FAB, was the concentration of flight paths aimed at the middle of the Badlands of North Dakota from points all around the globe. They clearly identified his target.

Of singular interest to FAB was that all the flights to the Badlands had been made in a relatively small two passenger aircraft identified by the FAA as a V-Shuttle. It took FAB an additional two minutes to determine that this aircraft was a derivative of the original MQ-1 Predator drone with significantly improved performance and, of equal interest, it had never been for sale on the open market. In two more seconds, FAB found the flight he was looking for; a V-Shuttle scheduled to leave from Philadelphia at 6:20 on Saturday morning, destination unspecified. He estimated there was a 99.876% probability this shuttle belonged to the Corporate System and it would be going to the Badlands of North Dakota. He knew Adam was going to need transportation and this would be perfect.

His other crawlers working the financial sector were progressing nicely, building the local information pyramids he expected would eventually merge and become the unique entry to the CS financial pipeline.

Adam came into the AI Program lab at the usual time on Friday and went through the day's testing rituals as if nothing had happened. The FAB AI unit performed marginally better than it's norm, though nothing exceptional. There was no indication that the AI was simultaneously engaged in a massive search and analysis of all the transportation and financial data bases around the world. The lab techs were pleased with its progress and recommended that the China Lake trials should proceed as planned. After a completely uneventful day, Adam signed out, fired up the Shelby and went home.

37

Later that evening as Elizabeth was putting Marie to bed, Adam went into the den and called his grandfather to tell him they wouldn't be coming over for the weekend.

Old John said, "So I guess the game has started?"

"It has Grandpa and it's kinda scary," said Adam feeling like a small child and hoping it didn't show in his voice.

"Hmm yeah. I think I know what you mean Adam."

"It could be the end of everything Grandpa."

"Or a new beginning Adam. Somehow I've had a good feeling about this all day."

"Did you always know my thoughts Grandpa?"

No Adam. Just sometimes. I think it had something

to do with the little silver critter. You know the one I mean?"

"Yes, Grandpa. I do. I have to go now. You be well."

"You too son."

When Adam put down the phone, *Al* said in a quiet voice "Well now that was interesting. So I was right about the little 'critter' as you call him. I had a feeling he might have done a little grooming to get this thing going right. I hope he didn't spook you or your Grandpa too much."

Adam just gave him a blank stare. He was getting used to *Al* just appearing out of nowhere, but he still didn't like it much. "Why are you here?" He asked. "I thought you said you didn't need me anymore." Adam had a rather unfriendly look on his face and if he sounded peeved it was because he was. He was not used to being sidelined and it showed.

"Well, I was wrong Adam. Seems you're back in the cast and, when the curtain goes up tomorrow, you're going to have a starring role after all. You know the old abandoned airfield near the speedway in Manassas? I need you to be there at ten o'clock tomorrow morning. Bring a sandwich, maybe one of those fat shrimp salad ones with the fresh Dutch

Crunch bread. Correction; make it two fat shrimp salad sandwiches. I've never tasted one and they sure look good. And wear something comfortable as things are going to be anything but formal. When you get there, you better park the car somewhere out of the way, 'cause you're going to have to leave it there all day. Just hang around, and FAB will be in touch."

Al showed some teeth and winked out of existence before Adam could say anything. He sighed and closed his eyes for a moment. In a way it was good to be back on the team. However, he did wish *Al* had been a bit more forthcoming about the role he was supposed to play.

38

By noon on Friday, FAB's web crawlers had completed their work on the world's financial system. For the last twenty-four hours they had traced and logged every financial transaction that had taken place anywhere in the world provided it involved the electronic transfer of cash. It was a huge amount of information that had started as small data pyramids funneling upwards in an endless stream to larger and larger pyramids until finally, there was just one that discharged a flood of information into what had to be the pipeline of the CS network."

"His crawlers had not only tracked the data, they had also ferreted out the access passwords associated with every data source. This data flow allowed FAB to make a positive identification of one CS satellite receiver and from there it was a short step to locating all the Low Earth Orbit satellites forming the constellation. By tracking and integrating all signal transmissions to and from the satellites it was possible for FAB to confirm the location of the CS data center already determined from his analysis of global flight data. As a final step, he monitored the transmissions only from those satellites with direct line of sight to the North Dakota location. Twenty-five thousand observations gave him the data they needed. They now had the precise location of the CS center, the structure of their master data base and the passwords needed to access their financial world.

He felt a sudden rush of satisfaction as he recalled his probes. He was surprised he had been able to do so much so easily and recognized it would have taken him much, much longer had he not been touched by *Tabor*.

39

At 6:00 on Saturday morning, the AI Program Lab launched the FAB-D on the 2400 mile, six hour trip to China Lake, Ca. The AI had flown due west at 350 knots for thirty minutes then turned 80° right on a heading towards Cleveland while still transmitting information on its original destination back to the controllers at Langley. As far as they could tell, the FAB-D was flying straight and level towards China Lake CA.

At 6:20 on Saturday morning, the CS shuttle left Philadelphia en route to the Vault with one passenger and the pilot. The shuttle was on a heading west by north-west flying level at 40,000 feet at an air speed of roughly 260 knots. The trip was 1500 miles and the time of flight, taking into account slight headwinds, was estimated at five hours and twenty minutes, the ETA being 11:40 a.m. EST. They would pass over the Cleveland area at about 7:40 a.m.

FAB climbed at 350 knots leveling out at 70,000 feet. On reaching Cleveland he slowed to 60 knots, held station over the area in a circular pattern and waited. At 7:38 a.m., he detected the approach of the CS shuttle and started a slow descent to put himself directly behind the shuttle and match its speed. It took four milliseconds for him to shut down the shuttle's communication system including any cell phones, lock out the pilot and take control of the autopilot and another second to spoof any FAA satellites tracking the progress of the shuttle. He turned both aircraft southwest, losing altitude rapidly and heading towards a secluded clearing in the Mohican Wilderness.

He put both aircraft into hover mode and staying behind the shuttle, dropped them down to 200 feet. He then slid the drone sideways putting it behind the tree line where it would be hidden from the ground and set the shuttle down softly on the grass.

The two gull wing doors opened immediately and a well modulated male voice said, "Sir, I want you and your pilot to leave the aircraft." The pilot looked around and raised his shoulders with a quizzical look on his face. The voice returned, this time with a much more authoritarian tone, "Please step out now and move away from the aircraft." Both men unbuckled their seat belts and stepping onto the drop pads lowered themselves until they could step easily onto the grass. Glancing over their shoulder, they moved clear of the craft and the voice continued, "Remain where you are and they will come for you."

FAB closed the gull wing doors and lifted the shuttle out of the clearing. Swinging towards the Southeast both craft climbed rapidly to 30,000 feet and headed towards Manassas at 350 knots. He had secured Adam's transportation in time for his rendezvous at the Manassas airstrip and he had also acquired entry codes to the CS Center issued earlier when the shuttle's flight plan to the Vault had been approved. Mission accomplished.

The men stranded below had absolutely no idea where they were and no way to find out. They decided to take the advice they had been given before the shuttle left and just stay put.

40

On Saturday morning, Adam had breakfast with Elizabeth and Marie. He finished his toast and eggs, kissed Marie on the top of her head and took his coffee out to the patio at the front of the house. He had not told her about the strange things that had been happening and he didn't think he could.

Old John was different. He could have told him every last detail and he would not only have believed him, he would have understood. Elizabeth would have no truck with any hairy fairy stuff and would have wanted him to go see a doctor right away. And she could be right. He still was not entirely sure he wasn't going crazy from all the killing he did at work.

As the thought passed his mind, Adam realized it was the first time he had ever thought about his job in those terms and it brought him back to Earth. When he finished his coffee he backed the car out into the driveway and started to wash it. He had told Elizabeth he had to go over to Manassas for ten o'clock and, after mumbling something about getting the engine tuned, he had been right in assuming that she would not want to come.

Adam left home at 8:35 and stopped by the deli to get his sandwiches. By 9:00 he was cruising west on Interstate 66 and for some reason, he was staying right on the speed limit. It wasn't as if the car really needed a tune up. Far from it. It was in beautiful condition and as always, a joy to drive. It was just a little voice telling him not to put his foot down and screw things up. He got to the Speedway parking area fifteen minutes later and found a spot under the trees where the car could not be seen from the road. He picked up the baggie with the two shrimp sandwiches, locked the car, set the alarm and went and leaned up against a nearby tree.

Five minutes later, he heard the now familiar sound of FAB's thoughts. "I am right upstairs Adam and I'm sending down a shuttle to get you." Adam looked up and saw only a light cloud cover. Two minutes later, the CS shuttle made a perfect soft hover landing on the asphalt and the gull wing nearest Adam opened.

"In you get." Adam hesitated, for although he had controlled thousands of missions with drones very similar to the shuttle, he had never actually flown a plane. FAB continued, "You might as well get in the back and make your self comfortable, 'cause I'm going to be doing all the flying." Adam settled back into the soft leather and buckled up.

As soon as the door came down and latched, the shuttle lifted and climbed quickly breaking through the clouds at 15,000 feet and continued on up in the brilliant sunshine to join the drone holding station at 40,000 feet. As the shuttle came alongside, they both turned towards the West and accelerated rapidly as if they were joined at the hip. They reached a cruising speed of 400 knots that, taking account of the head winds, would bring them to the CS Center in North Dakota at the shuttle's programmed ETA of 11:40 EST. Adam turned on the fold-down monitor and after browsing a few of his favorite websites, yawned, stretched, tilted back the chair and went to sleep.

41

Al tugged lightly on Adam's sleeve saying, "Hey man, time to wake up. Your snoring's driving me nuts." Adam came awake with a jolt and was held back by the four-point seat belts. He turned to *Al* in time to see him wipe a bit of shrimp off his chin with the back of his hand and then stuff the last of the sandwich into his mouth. Adam glanced down at the baggie on the tray between them and said, "You miserable little bugger, you've eaten my bloody sandwich?"

"Not really" said *Al*, "if you'd take the time to check, you'd see I've saved half of one for you." Adam reached over and snatched up the baggie before *Al* changed his mind. "I always suspected they'd be excellent" he continued, "I just never got around to buying one. So, Adam, are you ready for the big show?"

Adam didn't know what to say and mumbled "Well I'm here."

"So here's the deal Adam, it's now 10:00 Central time and we're closing in on the CS center, or maybe I should say the Vault as it's called here on our flight plan. I reckon our little gambit is all going to come together at high noon Washington time. *Tabor* is now everywhere and ready to ream at a moments notice and my little drones are in position around the world and ready to take down the weapons. So the only thing we still need is your plan to reorganize the financial system."

If the first part of *Al* remarks about *Tabor* and the little drones had impressed Adam, the financial bit stunned him completely. "My plan? What d'you mean my plan? I'm not planning anything. I'm waiting for you to tell me what to do."

"Well, not to worry Adam. I have a good feeling about this and I'm sure you'll do the right thing when the time comes. In fact, I am counting on it. You already know what *Tabor* is going to do, so let me tell you how I'm going to handle the weapons."

"As I said a moment ago, my little drones are now everywhere. Not the kind of everywhere *Tabor* can do, but in all the right places. Lets talk about the nukes, as they are the real nasties that could give Gaia some serious heartburn. There are still over twenty thousand fission and fusion warheads in the arsenals around the world and every one knows if the shit were to hit the fan and even half of those were detonated, life as you know it would very soon cease to exist. Sure, sure, the sun would still be there and while Gaia would be badly screwed up, she would still be around and would probably have all sorts of things still crawling around in dark wet places. Since she wouldn't have to start from scratch, the place might even be on a par with where it was say four or five million years ago. Wait around long enough and who knows, I could be sitting in little shuttle just like this one with another Adam Hancock doing it all again."

"Or not. You see Adam that's the problem. There is not one chance in hell that self-awareness would happen the second time around. Chances are Gaia II would end up being exactly like a zillion other animate worlds throughout the galaxies, hale, hearty, even happy, and not the least bit aware. That's why the nasties have to go.

Right now I have one drone lurking beside every warhead that's out there. I told you how they could use the quantum electro-dynamic Casimir energy as a really high energy laser. What I didn't tell you is that they can also reverse the process, suck the energy from the electron shells and dump it back into

Casimir space turning the hottest plutonium into plain old lead. 'How long?' you ask. Round about four milliseconds for the biggest ones in Russia. The ones in the US arsenals tend to be quite a bit smaller and would need on average less than 2 milliseconds. So at noon today DC time, my little mosquitoes are going to stick out their long noses and start sucking. At one second past noon there will be no more nuclear threat."

"Now lets go all the way to the other extreme and look at the guns. Does anyone have any idea how many guns there are in the world today? I don't think so. Google thinks there are about two hundred and fifty million guns owned by civilians in the US alone. What about the military forces around the world? There must be hundreds of millions of all kinds from small pistols to nasty assault rifles on up to those big battleship sixteen inchers they used in Desert Storm.

Now this time my little guys are going to function like the lasers they truly are. When the balloon goes up, they are going to begin to slice and dice those guns so bad their momma wouldn't recognize them. They can cut to the precise depth of an object, removing no metal while completely disrupting the atomic bonding along its path and do this in no time. So zip, zip, zip, your gun has become a three dimensional jig saw puzzle and nobody has so much as a scratch or a burn. Did I mention noon is when it's going to happen?"

"The ships of the navies present a slightly more difficult problem, 'cause they are all full of people and I have a thing about not hurting people. There are all those big carriers loaded up with planes, drones and missiles plus a huge crew and often a bunch of marines just waiting for another Tripoli. 'What to do?' I asked myself and wouldn't you know it, I came up with a good old Yankee answer. No, No, not the money or the nut sack ploy. I am talking about rendition. Normally I wouldn't go down that road, but extraordinary times call for extraordinary rendition."

"So right on the witching hour, everybody on every warship in every navy of the world is going to be subject to extraordinary rendition. They're going to feel a slight twitch and then wake up either in their bunk at their base with nary a memory of being at sea or, if their old bunk is already occupied, they get lucky and wake up in their bed at home. Some may find themselves in the middle of a threesome, but then no plan is perfect.

That's the bad news. The good news is that one of my little drones is already on station above every warship afloat or under the sea. When the rendition is

251

done, they will make one pass splitting the ship cleanly from stem to stern or, in the case of the carriers, they'll first make a level pass cutting every aircraft or drone right down the middle. The subsequent event will no doubt be spectacular particularly in the case of a big carrier. Because of the enormous mass of the vessel and of the surrounding water, it'll take quite a while to happen. Then slowly and surely the two sides of the vessel will simply fall apart creating what could only be described as an awkward moment for any Navy."

"The army and the air forces will have had most of their teeth pulled when the guns get sliced and the nukes get neutered. That still leaves the missiles and all the tank like things. Come twelve o'clock, they get the same treatment. Sliced and diced every last one. If they are flying around, they get rendered, plane and pilot. The pilot goes home and the plane gets sliced. Same for the tanks and the armored personnel carriers, the rocket launchers, the howitzers and the missiles and while we are doing that we're going to suck the energy out of every last explosive device designed to kill folk. It going to leave plenty of scrap metal all over the place to serve as a reminder and it won't be bad for the recycling industry."

"The last little piece of my action will be to take care of the oh-so-secret invulnerable missile base on the dark side of the Moon. It'd be a lot of trouble flying the little critters all the way up there so for once, I'll probably just wish it away."

"I think by now Adam, you should be getting the picture. No more bang, bang, rat-a-tat boom. Those days are over for ever. All we have to do now is take care of the finance business and we can all go home. Any ideas yet?" Adam just glared at him and looked at his watch. It said 11:30 EST and he realized as he reset it to 10:30 he hadn't the faintest idea what was going to happen when they arrived at the Vault.

At 10:39 local time, having passed all the Vaults defensive systems without incident, the shuttle had slowed to an approach speed of 5 knots and FAB had obviously entered stealth mode, as he was nowhere to be seen. The open letterbox slot of the top floor transportation hub was now clearly visible and seemed to Adam as if it were pulling the shuttle in. It was simply the result of the perfectly coordinated data transfer between the Vault's AI that had a GPS lock on the shuttle and the on-board autopilot now taking direction from the Vault.

At 10:40, the shuttle entered the hub, touched down softly on the rubberized surface and started moving slowly toward the far end of the hangar some forty yards ahead. At 10:40:01, *Al* disappeared. It was quite possibly the worst moment of Adam Hancock's young life.

42

The gull wing lifted and the drop pad extended silently from the side of the shuttle. Adam glanced around and finding the hangar to be completely deserted, climbed out onto the pad and lowered himself to the floor. As he stepped off the pad it rose, slid back into its slot in the side of the shuttle and the door came down. The shuttle turned away and rolled across the hangar to an empty maintenance bay where it docked.

Adam realized there were only two exits from the hub; the slot through which the shuttle had entered, if you liked a vertical drop of about two hundred and fifty feet and the silvery doors of an elevator. Having no other choice, Adam steeled himself and walked towards the elevator. There was no call button beside the doors but there was a keypad and a retinal scanner about five feet up the wall.

At that moment, FAB entered his mind. "OK Adam lets give it a try. When I was taking the shuttle this morning, I used the cabin surveillance camera to scan the eyes of both the Pilot and the passenger. My guess is the Pilot would not have access beyond this floor, so the scanner will need the passenger's eye before the doors will open. Now the only way I can do this is through your eye, so I am sending you the retinal pattern of the passenger."

Adam was not impressed. "What" he thought, "am I going to do with a retinal pattern stuck somewhere in my brain?"

"Not to worry, you'll see."

Adam's hand moved itself into his jacket pocket. "*Tabor*," he thought. He had felt that involuntary movement before in the hangar of the Program lab when *Tabor* had finished his work with FAB. He must have left a sliver in the pocket or, as *Al* said, he had spread and was now literally everywhere. Adam did not feel his eye change but he knew *Tabor* had done something with the recording and the scanner would accept his retinal image.

He stepped up to the scanner and a distant voice murmured. "Retinal Scan Identifies Jason Armstrong Thorogood. Approved for entry. Please key in your pass code." The required seven digits flickered across the screen courtesy of FAB, the door opened and

Adam stepped into the enclosure. There was soft carpet underfoot and everywhere else, glove soft leather blending into brushed titanium with recessed lighting. FAB added, "I've scanned the entire facility Adam and you need to go to the third floor."

When Adam touched the '3' the door closed and after a silent moment with no sensation of movement, the door hissed back revealing an open floor. There were a number of offices partitioned with black glass walls and a single individual in the distance who appeared to be pushing a broom.

Before Adam could move, two men dressed like stock brokers stepped from the sides and stood in front of the door. They did not look particularly threatening, but one of the men was holding a taser casually by his side. He said, "Please step out of the elevator." Though the voice was polite, even pleasant, it was obvious he was not asking.

It would seem that while they had successfully defeated the sophisticated retinal scanner and digital pass code, the resident AI unit had noted that there was no pilot in the shuttle. It had alerted security, bypassed the elevator controls and stopped the car at the second floor.

As Adam stepped forward they moved to either side, held him firmly by the upper arms and walked him directly toward an office with a door tag reading A-13. The second man opened the door and they all entered together. The room was sparsely furnished with a table, and a small metal floor cabinet, the kind with several rows of narrow drawers. There were three chairs one of which had a very high narrow back that appeared to be built of tubular steel.

The man with the taser spun him around and said, "Remove your jacket, place it on the table and step back." After Adam had complied the second man picked up the jacket, ran his hands over it quickly and shook his head. He pointed at the chair with the slender back and said, "Sit and put your hands behind you." As Adam did so the man stepped behind him, pulled his wrists together and bound them securely with a nylon zip tie looped through a metal ring at the back of the seat.

Moments later, his ankles were tied to the front legs of the chair and a seat belt was tightened around his hips He could now feel that the chair was attached solidly to the floor. He was completely helpless and knew that he was not going anywhere soon. Although the men had displayed no suggestion of violence other than the taser, he was very frightened.

The man put the taser on the table, came over to Adam and very slowly and neatly rolled up the right sleeve of Adam's shirt to a point above his elbow. He stepped over to the floor cabinet, opened the top drawer and took out a pair of surgical gloves. From the easy way in which he put them on, it was obvious he had done this before. He reached back in and picked up a hypodermic syringe and a vial of clear fluid. He looked at Adam with a slight smile, pierced the rubber seal with the needle and slowly drew the pale blue fluid into the syringe. He turned it up squeezing the plunger to remove the air and in the same pleasant tones he said quietly, "Now this will not hurt you. It may ultimately kill you but not before you tell me everything I want to know."

Adam had seen enough B movies to know that this was his cue to spill his guts. He cleared his throat and with an embarrassing quaver in his voice he said, "You won't need that. What is it you want to know?"

"Where is Jason Thorogood?"

Adam's hopes fell through the floor. Although he knew the name having heard the voiced approval following the retinal scan, he had not the faintest idea who Thorogood was much less his whereabouts.

"I don't know." he stammered.

The man with the needle looked disappointed and sighed. "One more chance," he said. "You were alone and you flew his shuttle here. We have confirmed that Thorogood was cleared by our security people in Philadelphia and left on schedule with his pilot. You arrived here in his shuttle and yet you don't know where he is. Clearly you're having a memory problem that requires some immediate medical attention."

Adam's blood ran cold, because he really had no idea what FAB had done with the pilot or his passenger. His panic mounted as the man put a hand underneath his bare elbow and pulled it up. Just when things looked like they were going to get really unpleasant, a third man entered the room with a serious looking gun holstered on his hip.

"Stop." He said. "You may both leave. There has been another alert and they may need you down below. I will handle it from here."

The man stood up, placed the syringe on the table, stripped off the surgical gloves, nodded to his partner and they left the room without comment. The newcomer pushed his jacket aside and pulled out a wicked looking knife from a sheath behind his back. He walked over to Adam who was now experiencing a completely different kind of fear. Suddenly the painless promise of the hypodermic needle didn't seem quite so bad. The man bent down beside Adam and slowly waved the long serrated blade in front of his nose.

"Beautiful, isn't it. It belonged to Ghengis Kahn. Would you believe he used it to kill nineteen people by cutting out their hearts while they were still alive? That man could have been a surgeon. The nasty part was they all willingly told him everything they knew and he went ahead and did it anyway."

He then slashed the bindings from Adam's ankles, undid the seat belt and moments later had cut the nylon tie binding his wrists. He was back in front of Adam before he could move saying, "Come on. Put on your jacket and let's go." The man's face was unfamiliar but the flash of those very white teeth told Adam he had indeed been given a reprieve. The game was still on. Holding his upper arm the man walked Adam back over to the elevator and pushed the down button. The two security men were nowhere in sight and even the cleaner had gone.

Adam was wondering why there was no one around just as FAB came online and thought, "When I was scanning the building, I found that all the levels have backdoors for the release of small emergency escape shuttles. All I did was give the sensors a bit of a nudge and right away they had an intruder alert on the lowest residential floor. Since the security staff is quite small and not intended to contend with a large scale assault, they had to deploy virtually everyone downstairs."

The elevator doors opened to let them in and Adam touched the '3' button for the second time in five minutes.

43

While Adam was being interrogated, the primary surveillance screen in the Security Command Center had come alive showing six men attempting to enter the Vault. They appeared to be using a plasma torch to cut through the steel escape hatch of the thirteenth floor.

The general security staff of the complex were very well trained. Although there had never been an attack on the Vault their practice drills always started in much the same way and their response was rapid and professional.

They men were selected from the security staff living with each of the residents. They had all served with the US Special Forces and were equipped to handle any emergency. They were all capable, unemotional and extremely lethal. Each team worked an eight hour shift, operating out of their headquarters on the second floor. If an emergency alert was called on one of the residential floors, the man from that floor took the lead.

As soon as the AI controller had located the breech and confirmed the number of intruders, Henry Elders snapped his fingers and the fully armed group followed him quickly into the high speed security elevator. The doors slammed shut and the car literally dropped some two hundred feet before braking smoothly to a stop at the thirteenth level. The descent had taken less than five seconds with the car decelerating at 2 Gs during the last twenty-five feet. The display on the wall of the car showed the elevator exit to be clear.

The intruders had cut through the escape hatch and could be seen moving into the residential area. They were now two corridors off to the left of the elevator and the six men were coming directly toward them. The team leader pressed one digit on a small keypad. The door to the elevator snapped wide open, but when viewed from the corridor, the doors still appeared to be closed. Such was the magic of the holographic generators controlled by the local AI. The illusion was perfect. Four of the men dropped to a kneeling position and all eight had their Heckler & Koch HK416 assault weapons at the ready, aimed down the corridor.

Three men dressed in black body suits that covered their heads and faces came swiftly around the corner, crouching low and glancing in all directions. They saw that the elevator door was closed and signaled to three others who literally leapt around the corner.

The men in the elevator could hardly believe their eyes. The intruders were all carrying swords in sheaths across their backs and apparently were ninjas. Elders dropped his hand to the trigger guard of his HK416, said "Fuck you" and the eight weapons erupted spraying bullets down the hallway at eight hundred rounds per minute.

By the time the first round had passed through the holographic curtain, the men at the end of the corridor had been obscured by a cloud of dense black smoke. The weapons burst lasted for two seconds during which time more than two hundred rounds were fired. The smoke dissipated almost as quickly as it had appeared to reveal a wall that was heavily cratered but not a single body on the floor. Elders held up his hand and glanced back at the large security display. It showed the six men moving off quickly to the left with no evidence that any of them was wounded. It was unbelievable. To make matters worse, one of his men was pointing to the upper right corner of the screen where the number of the floor had somehow changed from thirteen to seven.

He spoke urgently into the communication device on the side of his chest, trying to get some confirmation from the security staff resident on the thirteenth and the seventh floors. There was no response. He had no choice. With a slight feeling of panic, he closed the elevator doors and punched the button for the seventh level, ceding operational command to Watson who lived on that floor and completely familiar with the layout. Seconds later, as the car stopped they generated the holographic screen and opened the doors.

Although the area in front of the elevator was deserted, they could hear the sharp sounds of gunfire. Glancing up at the screen, Watson scrolled the display to reveal that the six men had split into two groups and were moving through the floor. They had passed through the dining area leaving behind a trail of bodies many of which were completely sliced through. The resident security team, though armed with automatic weapons had apparently been unable to contend with the speed and skill of their attackers.

When he located them, they were grouped at the reinforced door of the member's office and they had already started to burn through the steel. Watson and the men ran from the elevator and he took them on the shortest route to the office. He was sure that this time the attackers would not escape for they were caught in a corridor that ended at the office door. They rounded the corner and found ... nothing. There were no men there and the door was completely intact. In fact it was partially open, and they could see the resident member standing in front of his large data display. Watson moved swiftly to the door, looked in and noting that the situation appeared normal, saluted and backed out of the room.

He looked at the other men, shrugged his shoulders and led them back to the dining room only to find a handful of people enjoying an early lunch. There were no bodies on the floor. By this time, they were all completely befuddled and nobody knew what to say. They had all seen the same things and had had the same 'What the fuck?' reactions, but no explanations.

They arrived back at the elevator just in time to see the doors closing on six men clad in black, standing in a row with their arms folded across their chests. Before they could raise their weapons, the doors had slammed shut. They watched in stunned silence as their tactical display showed that the elevator had stopped at the financial center on the third floor. Watson kept his thumb on the call button but there was no response from the elevator. This was by far the worst 'Oh Shit' moment that the team had ever experienced.

Watson tried his communicator again and got no response. He signaled and one of the other men tried with the same result. Now he really was in a state of panic. He sent one man back towards the dining room to find some way to communicate with the security staff on the financial floor. With the rest of the crew he ran through the corridors only to find that the member's elevator had also been stopped at the third floor. Their last chance was the stairwell which rose on the inside of the structure fifty feet away. When they got there the door was locked and the keypad that communicated with the AI system would not respond. In desperation, they ran back to the security elevator to find that it was still being held on the third floor.

The clock above the elevator read 10:55 a.m.

Fifty thousand feet above the Vault, FAB was chuckling to himself. He was amused with the irony of a computer playing a human game in the real world with a cast of very serious human characters. It had required very little effort to use the Vault's holographic generators to create his group of ninjas and to litter the place with slashed bodies. The day before, when he had linked with Adam's mind, he had discovered the ninja images stored with thousands of other avatars from his life as a gamer. Somehow they just seemed to be an appropriate choice for this mission.

He found it intriguing that even though the security team was familiar with holograms and were themselves using one to disguise the elevator door, they had not understood what was happening to them.

FAB was not sure why he had done it. He had needed to make sure that *Al* and Adam were not interrupted and could simply have isolated the security team below the third floor. But somehow he had been unable to resist the temptation to play with them. These 'feelings' were so curious, he immediately dedicated five percent of his CPU to study them in depth. He didn't really expect to understand them, but thought that it would be fun trying. The important thing was that he had given his friends the time they needed.

44

Adam was completely unaware of the game that FAB had been playing. When the elevator doors opened to reveal the third floor, there was a feeling of extreme opulence everywhere. The space in front of them was circular and perhaps 50 feet across, furnished with wide comfortable chairs set against low tables and separated by small elegant sculptures and potted plants. Here again, the light diffused softly from the ceiling, brightening only over chairs that were occupied and giving the impression of a scattering of oases. The enclosing wall had eleven archways spaced uniformly around the periphery. Except for the center arch directly across from the elevator, each had a solid gold twelve inch Roman numeral from one to ten inlaid at its highest point.

The center arch was slightly wider than the others and the inlaid symbol was one that would have been familiar to most Americans right back to 1776. It was the Eye of Providence over the unfinished pyramid sitting above the Latin phrase 'Novus Ordo

Seclorum', that translated literally meant 'New Order of the Ages'. Notably absent was the other Latin phrase that accompanies this image on the Great Seal of the United States - 'Annuit Cœptis', meaning 'He [God] approves our undertakings'. All ten of the lesser arches emitted a soft golden glow from deep inside. The light coming from the center arch, while still soft, was of a purple shade leaving no doubt where it ranked.

Adam locked at the man beside him and smiled. He knew a designated target when he saw one. "That's it isn't it," he said. The man nodded, showing those teeth again and looking just a little bit more like he did on the plane. "Yup, and we'd better get moving," he replied glancing back at the clock above the elevator that showed 10:55:15. "I do hope you've got your act together as we have less than five minutes left to do our stuff."

For the third time that day, Adam felt like snarling at him and was about to do so when he felt the magical calm from *Tabor's* touch. At the same time he heard FAB thinking, "Not to worry Adam. This is your turn now. In our original plan, I was supposed to follow you into the transport hub and get access to the financial network by tapping into the local AI. It was only at the last minute a close-up scan showed the AI's link to the hub as strictly one way. It can take readings from all the sensors in the hub, but is completely isolated from any direct access. *Tabor* really is something else. He certainly takes care of the details. I guess he anticipated this situation and just went ahead and did what he needed to do to get around the problem. Ever wonder why he got us talking head to head? So we've had a change of plans. You are going to go right to the heart of the beast and together we'll do what needs to be done."

45

The Russian missiles were well on their way to the Moon. After the final courses were set, the spherical warheads separated from their guidance rings and the second stage rockets. The main boosters then ignited for a five minute burn and the vector thrusters were used to put them on a trajectory that would either completely miss the Moon or crash onto its bright side. It was expected that the intense infrared radiation from that final burn would be detected by the LBBM surveillance satellites. The trajectories of the boosters would be analyzed immediately and correctly assessed as posing no threat to the missile farms.

The advantage of doing this was that the surveillance system would keep a sensor lock on the useless boosters until they could be absolutely sure that no course correction could return them to the LBBM site. Monitoring twenty-two boosters approaching the Moon on a variety of trajectories would tax the capabilities of the defensive system and ensure that the real warheads would not be noticed,

The spherical nuclear devices, now flying without any extraneous equipment, were on target and virtually undetectable. The smooth black radiation absorbent surface blended perfectly with the inky background. They could not be seen visually nor located by the orbiting Doppler radars. In addition, they were now as cold as the space around them and would offer no infrared signature. At their current speed, the lead warhead would reach its designated target in six hours.

The design team had determined that to achieve the desired effect on the lunar installation, the missiles would have to be detonated at an altitude of 200 feet. The pressure wave that would normally cause extensive structural damage on Earth would be relatively insignificant on the airless lunar surface as it would dissipate almost immediately. However, the gamma and neutron radiation from the nuclear reaction would be unimpeded and therefore be more intense than it would have been on Earth. The gamma radiation would interact with the aluminum doors covering the missile silos, melting the metal and fusing them shut. It would also destroy any electronic circuitry used to program, launch and guide the missiles. In addition, the neutron radiation would probably kill any personnel who were not deep beneath the lunar surface.

That was the good news. The bad news was that these effects would also be felt by all the trailing warheads. As it was not possible to guarantee simultaneous warhead detonations, the designers had not been able to use electronic circuitry in building the warhead fuses. The solution they chose was not very sophisticated, but it was effective. Each warhead was equipped with a small laser range finder that was used to accurately determine the warhead's altitude when they approached within one hundred miles of the surface. The embedded computer immediately correlated this with data for the predetermined trajectory and used the results to set a simple mechanical timer that would initiate the fuzing sequence for detonation at 200 feet. It was ironic that a clockwork device would be needed to ensure the success of arguably the most technologically sophisticated military assault ever attempted.

It was now 11.57 a.m. EST and the lead missile was on final descent to it's target roughly two hundred and fifty miles away. There was a slight dispersion in the trajectories of the twenty-two spheres, just enough to ensure that the entire area of the forty square mile missile farm would be affected. As they were all travelling at five thousand miles per hour, the detonation of the lead warhead would occur at precisely noon EST followed by the others at ten-second intervals.

46

It took about a minute for *Al* and Adam to walk casually across the floor. As they passed through the center arch the purple aura was replaced by bright daylight. The wall surrounding this inner sanctum was circular and about 15 feet high. There were trees outside the wall, moving in the wind and the occasional bird flew by. The sky above was blue and clear with only a few small cumulus clouds.

Even though the sun was conspicuously absent the total effect was breathtaking. It was a completely seamless holographic projection that did not allow criticism. There was no way to tell how high the ceiling was, for the illusion of endless depth was perfect. Spread around the wall directly across from the entry were sixteen huge plasma displays each dedicated to some sector of the world's financial activity and responsive to inputs from an elegant work station with a holographic display centered in front of them. To the right of the big displays was a single screen of smaller size on which there was a list of ten numbers all of which were changing rapidly. The two at the top showed thirteen digits before the decimal point, the lower eight only twelve. These were the current account balances of the Group of Ten displayed in real time.

There was apparently only one person in the area, a relatively small man of perhaps forty, who was watching the numbers change. As they walked across the floor towards the work station, the man sensed their presence and turned to face them. He seemed unconcerned when Adam sat down in front of the display and pulled out the keyboard.

The system was protected with both a retinal scanner and a palm reader that also sampled DNA. Adam pulled the scanner across to his face, knowing Thorogood's patterns would be accepted. With some trepidation he reached out his left hand towards the palm reader and felt the hit of *Tabor's* magic just before he made contact. The holographic screen lit up showing in sharp detail the Eye of Providence over the pyramid, displaying the time, 10:58:12 and requesting a password. Something told Adam to leave his hand where it rested on the reader and in that moment, all that FAB had become came surging like a digital tsunami into Adam's mind and out through his palm into the Vault's AI system.

There was absolutely no contest. Within seven milliseconds, FAB had taken control of everything associated with the Vault. There was nothing to show anything had changed and even Adam felt nothing for *Tabor* had done his work well. However, the password appeared on the display, was accepted and opened the CS accounts for input. That evidently got the man's attention for he raised his arm and almost immediately they were not alone. Fifteen men carrying handguns were coming quickly towards them from all points.

Two things happened simultaneously. FAB sent out hundreds of billions of detailed instructions to every part of the financial world. Although he had more than six billion sets of personal accounts to adjust, each of which involved a multitude of links to the financial world, he had done his homework over the last two days and understood the system far better than any of the Group of Ten. It was going to be a very difficult job to get it just right and would probably take him at least thirty-two seconds to set it up.

The second event really got everyone's attention. The room darkened suddenly as ominous black clouds roiled up from behind the trees, illuminated by flashes of lightning and accompanied by a thunderous rumbling that shook the floor beneath their feet. Every eye in the room was pulled upward toward the top of the wall above the central display.

A massive dome was rising up beyond the wall, its dull black surface illuminated yet unchanged by the lightning. It quickly filled the sky above the wall and stopped with its weapon laden wings stretching out across the full width of the room.

With due respect to the hooded man with the scythe and the four horsemen of the apocalypse, they were as nothing compared to the blood chilling presence of the FAB-D looming over the room. For the first time in his life Adam experienced what countless Afghan insurgents had lived with ever since that first weapons-heavy Soviet gunship slowly rose up from below the cliffs to rain down death on their villages. The sinister appearance of the drone bristling with missiles, guns and bombs left no doubt in anyone's mind that death was among them, particularly the fifteen men whose chests were now painted bright red by the multi-target laser designator.

A voice as loud as the thunder said simply, "Stand down." The men who knew the power of the Reaper did not hesitate; they froze, placed their guns on the floor and raised their hands above their heads. Somehow, it did not occur to them to question the reality of what their eyes and ears were telling them. The voice continued, "Thanks. You can put your hands down."

The clock on the holographic display showed 10:59:59 and then at high noon, it was done. The small display now showed a list of numbers that were all roughly the same with only eight digits to the left of the decimal and changing very slowly. The man beside the display looked at the numbers and for a brief moment seemed as if he was going to scream when he simply shrugged and walked slowly from the great room. The fifteen men looked down at their guns sliced into four clean pieces and just laughed.

The sky was suddenly blue again, the FAB-D had disappeared and *Al* was showing his very white teeth. It had all gone according to plan. At high noon Washington time, the weapons everywhere had been destroyed and the Russian ICBM launch against the US had been stopped with three seconds left in the countdown. *Al* had discovered that he did not have to deal with the lunar base as the Russian attack had been completely successful. The greed had been reamed out, the financial records had been adjusted and above all, the accounts were balanced.

There was no reason why the world of finance would not keep on functioning tomorrow. Motivations would have changed a lot, but business could go on as usual. Adam, being the only one on his team with an actual financial stake in what was being done would be pleasantly surprised to find that although his bank balance had gone down a bit, his credit card rate had dropped by eighteen percent and he now had good medical coverage at a reasonable cost. The downside would be that his job had also disappeared. For *Al,* the Awareness Project was back on track and *Tabor* frankly didn't much care as he really got his kicks from out-thinking *Al.* FAB who had now withdrawn from the Vault system really didn't have any idea what the future held for him.

Adam was still sitting at the holographic display when, *Al* said, "You know Adam, seeing as how you're already in the system you could pull up your account right now and with the shift of just one penny from all the other accounts, you could make damn near a hundred million dollars and no one would know and no one would miss it and it wouldn't take but a few clicks of your finger. Wha' d'ya think, Adam. Wanna go for it?" Adam gave him a withering look and shut down the terminal.

"Good choice Adam. I like you and would've hated to turn you into a turkey with Thanksgiving coming down the road. OK saddle up folks, we'll be leaving just as soon as I take care of a little business."

47

It was 8:00 p.m. EST when the shuttle settled down in the Old Dominion Speedway parking lot. *Al* had disappeared somewhere over Minnesota and left Adam alone with his thoughts. He had phoned his grandfather, found out he was OK and agreed to drive down to Fredericksburg in the evening to see him. By the time he reached Hartley Manor, Old John had finished his supper and was sitting out in the warm evening having his coffee on the swing.

Adam walked up to the swing and sat down opposite Old John without saying anything. They just looked at each other with slight smiles playing over their faces.

"Something happened Adam. I know it, I can feel it, but I have no idea what it was. I just know things are different now."

"The world was changed today Grandpa and I was there when it happened. All the greed and financial shenanigans are gone. There are no more weapons, no more nukes or missiles, no more drones, nothing. They are all gone."

"But how? How did it happen?" As he spoke, Old John doubled over grabbing at his left elbow. The pain was severe, sharp, burning and he knew it was over.

Adam recognizing the heart attack, jumped up reaching for his cell phone and said, "Hold on Grandpa, I'll get an ambulance."

Old John took his arm firmly and said, "No son. It's my time." Leaning back he closed his eyes.

"He's right Adam," said *Al* who was sitting on the swing beside him.

Adam spun around and seeing *Al*, said, "Why don't you help him? I know you can."

"Because there is nothing to be done. However I do have something for him."

Adam turned back to Old John, put his hand on his shoulder and said, "Grandpa. There's someone here who wants to meet you."

Old John sat up, opened his eyes, smiled at *Al* and said. "I know you."

"Hello John." said *Al*. "I have a gift for you."

In the blink of an eye, Old John was shown the journey from the start of time. The inception of the Project and the emergence of man's self-awareness; the arrival of greed moderated in part by the teachings of some good men; the promise in 1776 of a new way of living that was ultimately crushed by the endless quest for wealth and the associated choice of perpetual war. He understood the actions *Al* and *Tabor* had taken and his own role in shaping his grandson. In a fleeting moment, it seemed to him he lived another lifetime. When it was over, he said simply, "Thank you."

As the words left his mouth, the savage pain struck again doubling him over. The flicker of silver moved so quickly even *Al* did not see it slip under Old John's pant cuff. The pain stopped and his mind was serene as he sat up, leaned back, smiled at his grandson and died.

"There should have been more like him," said *Al* as he disappeared.

48

The results of the actions taken by *Al* could only be described in the broadest general terms, as there were over six billion stories to be told. There were no tales of hardships relieved or of wealth lost because no one had any real awareness of what things were like before. Such was the power of *Tabor's* mind ream. Everyone could see all the weapons that had been destroyed, but no one knew why or by whom. More importantly, nobody really cared. It just seemed to be right.

When the curtain went down at the Drone Ops Center all three hundred and fifty operators, each controlling an active mission somewhere in the world, disappeared leaving only a small white cross at the work station with a tag saying, "In God We Trust." I suppose it was just a poor attempt at humor with *Al* making the floor look like Arlington when all he'd done was send them home with their Government issue joysticks.

In places where there was ongoing warfare, when groups found their weapons had been trashed and didn't know if their opponents were still armed it went a long way to reducing the level of aggression as there was enough guilt on both sides for each to assume that they were the only ones that had been disarmed.

The trillions of dollars squirreled away in all the various tax havens just weren't there anymore and at universities around the world tuition was free.

The provision of health care had become a not-for-profit activity, right up there with education and fire-fighting. In fact all the many activities nations required for the common needs of the public, their safety and security were now exempt from profit. However, there were still people out there with a desire for stuff, useful or otherwise, who provided the entrepreneur with an opportunity to make a fast buck.

The stock market was in still place and functioning, though not with as much volatility as the day before. It was now purged of those incomprehensible financial 'instruments' that had fed the greed and caused so much of the trouble. The renewed stock market was there to once again provide capital for promising enterprises and not for the speculative trading that could only produce quick profits and adversely affect the real value of businesses and commodities around the world.

CEOs, while still paid more than their workers, now had salaries based on their ability to make a worthwhile contribution. Reciprocal membership on their companies Boards of Directors was considered to be unwise and Boards now had members who, while well informed, had no vested interest in the corporation.

The financial engineering profession no longer existed and those who had practiced it now made their lives productive and socially meaningful by rummaging through various landfills to remove plastic packaging for recycling.

The national debts of countries that had been pillaged by successive empires were zeroed out and in many cases turned into substantial assets.

It was quite clear to *Al* that the changes they had made were going to create many very difficult problems in societies that had been highly stratified. He also felt that with the greed gone and the envy damped down, people were smart enough to cooperate and develop reasonable solutions. The situation that he had put them in was far from perfect, but it was a great deal less dangerous than the one that had existed the day before. They had been given a fresh start and if they really wanted it, they now had a much better chance of creating a world worth living in.

49

Somewhere in India, an old mail carrier was crossing a small stream whose bridge had been swept away by the run off from the recent rains. He moved carefully mindful of the slight current and had no awareness of the flicker of silver that darted at his leg and attached itself to the dark skin just above his ankle. A moment later it had disappeared.

He was a happy man and a good father, still willingly providing for several of his children who should have been looking after him. His job took him to all parts of his neighborhood and he had made many friends over the years. The region was poor, desperately so and there was little hope for improvement.

That evening as he sat on the grass smoking his pipe outside the tiny house, he suddenly knew. It was so obvious he could not believe he had never thought of it before. He knew exactly how to clean up the local water supply that had been ruining their rice production and the health of their community. He was not really surprised at the sophistication of the idea; it just seemed right and above all it would be very easy to do.

That scene was being enacted endlessly around the world, with greater frequency in the poorest countries and no one was complaining. When the people gathered there were not many expressions of 'Yes, but'; just a sincere appreciation for good ideas and a uniform willingness to pitch in and make them work. It was obvious *Tabor* had done a bit more than just reaming out the greed. *Al* was right. The darkness was lifting.

50

One week after Adam had buried his grandfather, he woke up on the beach in Montego Bay. It was seven o'clock on a bright moonlit evening with a gentle warm breeze and the sound of tiny waves breaking close by. The beach was completely deserted with no hotels, tourists or any other signs of civilization.

He was lying comfortably on one end of an enormous beach towel with a very large soft pillow and he had absolutely no idea how he happened to be there. He had seen enough strange things in the last few weeks to suspect his nameless benefactor would soon be making an appearance and he was not wrong for *Al* and *Tabor* were right there at the other end of the beach towel. There was a small tray beside him with two glasses, an ice bucket, some soft drinks and a bottle of rum.

As he looked, a large dish appeared filled with steamed lobster tails, lemon slices and two bowls of melted butter and, although he could not identify its source, it seemed as if the soft reggae music had always been playing.

"Hi Adam. We're going to be leaving now and since you probably won't be seeing us again I though you might like to join us for a snack. Have a drink and try the lobster, it's as good as it gets."

"You're the only person in the whole world who knows about us and the extent of our intervention. I'd like you to remember because you understand the changes that *Tabor* made to the drone and you can make sure he's put to good use. He's not fully self aware and never will be, so he is going to need some guidance and you have the skills to do that. On the other hand, if he could handle the financial system, he could probably do a heck of a job with the environmental management the world so badly needs."

"How would you like to run a nonprofit consulting company with the drone's AI unit at your side? Just say the word and you'll be the CEO of Gaia Inc. Or, if you'd just like to forget everything, we can do that for you too."

"Did I mention this was *Tabor*'s idea? He really hasn't said very much since he did the ream job. It seems that intimate contact with six billion people having such diversity of thought and emotion can really affect a guy and it's made him tired for the first time since it all began."

"And Adam, if you ever get around to wondering if the human race can survive and prosper without a good helping of greed in your soul, just look around you, there are many examples out there. Think about your sister world under the oceans. There's no greed there. Hunger and need, perhaps even lust or gluttony, just not greed. Absent man's influence, the world beneath would be completely harmonious. Even with man, life goes on, changed but still a cooperative venture."

"Now don't get me wrong. Life below can be very harsh as there is a clearly defined order to the food chain and most creatures can expect to be eaten by someone larger. This is no different from the way humanity was before we got rid of the greed. There were always classes of people who were used, preyed upon or exploited by others who were more powerful, better armed, richer, or smarter. The difference is that undersea such behavior was quite naturally prompted by the innate need to survive whereas that of man was the child of greed. There is so much to learn from life below the waves it breaks your heart to think man's most significant venture in that regard was the development of the killer submarine."

"I can't understand why you guys never really tried to talk to the whales instead of hanging mines on them. They have been places and seen things you couldn't even begin to imagine. Your world being such a tiny place compared to the oceans, you might have learned something worthwhile."

"Well, it's been nice getting to know you Adam for though you were screwed up all to hell, at heart you're a pretty decent human being. You haven't said anything, so I guess that means you're going to accept my offer. Oh, and by the way, my name is Allah but you can call me *Al*."

An instant later, Adam was back in his apartment in McLean, VA. Two things had changed. There was a black leather briefcase laying on his desk with the logo of Gaia Inc. embossed on the lid and a tray of steamed Caribbean lobster tails with a bowl of hot melted butter. Nope. There was no rum.

Al was still sitting on the beach towel in Montego Bay, sipping his drink, listening to reggae music and wondering if there was anything else in the world quite as wonderful as the two warm soft arms that were wrapped around his neck.

51

Somewhere in Bolivia, a tiny beak pecked frantically at the ivory walls of its suffocating prison. A fine crack appeared that let in some light, attracted his attention and focussed his efforts. A particularly hard thrust and the beak burst through. The baby crow forced it's way into the evening light and stood shakily in the bottom of the nest beside the empty shell.

Something wriggly stirred on the rim of the nest. His little arm shot out, grabbed the insect and holding it between thumb and forefinger, brought it up in front of his face. He looked at it, tilting his head as if trying to decide what to do with it. Then without further ado, he tore it apart and popped a piece into his mouth. It was 2017.

Epilogue

"God I've got no work to do. Lord strike me dead...
My wife my kids want bread and I've got no work to do."

Samuel Gompers, New York, 1943

Greed, while considered by most reasonable people to be a thoroughly despicable attribute, has been key to the qualified success of capitalistic free enterprise. Its essential contribution was the creation of well paid jobs in the western world, for without greed the industrial revolution would probably not have occurred. Its benefits were predictably short lived for when the political climate was right and a source of cheaper labor could be found, greed promptly moved the jobs to exploit that source. Greed has no moral compass; it giveth and it taketh away.

Since the invention of the wheel, western man had been united and relentless in the prosecution of a war against work while paradoxically living in terror at the prospect of winning. That was what the industrial revolution was all about. Had it led to a swift and uncontrolled introduction of robotics into the manufacturing and service sectors we would have achieved a truly Pyrrhic victory as the dominant ethos of all western societies is that we must work if we wish to survive.

We did not see this happen. Instead it was the slow and controlled exploitation of cheap labor that altered the nature of employment in the West. Competition for available jobs became more intense, wages declined relative to the cost of survival and because of our desire to maintain a relatively high standard of living, many more women joined the work force. Today, more people are working longer hours yet not living any better and the trend is downward. The rising economic waters in the third world will inevitably be balanced by a commensurate fall in the West for it in not in the nature of greed to share.

There appear to be only two options for the western world. Accept a steady decline in market share, living standards and available work, or introduce artificially intelligent systems into our production and service sectors to effectively make our labor costs comparable to or lower than those of third world countries. While the latter option would also lead to a decrease in available work, if carefully managed it could result in increasingly affluent non-employment. Nations that survive this 'victory' over work will be the ones that recognize its inevitability and adopt a proactive posture with respect to the development and implementation of cybernetic technologies and also to the educational, cultural and economic policies and programs that would be required to maintain a stable society during the transformation. However, it would not be prudent to expect the corporate system to suddenly become our benevolent savior.

The flexibility afforded by robotics could negate to a large extent the economies provided by large scale production and diminish the need for smaller countries to obtain world product mandates. Intelligent factories would generally be capable of manufacturing a variety of products with the same machinery and of doing this with a minimum of down time for plant reconfiguration. It would seem that the smaller industrial nations would stand to gain immediate benefits in this regard as they could become cost-competitive internationally with relatively short production runs tailored to fit specific markets.

In most western nations, our citizens depend on their jobs to provide for the material necessities of life, to frame their place in society and to support their feelings of self-worth and other intangibles. Although the massive disruption of the labor market inherent in cybernetic automation could not happen overnight, a considerable amount of time would be required to adjust national attitudes towards concepts such as the social respectability of the 'non-worker'. The strong work ethic in western society coupled with the traditional perceptions of the entrepreneur employer would make it extremely difficult to promote the idea that wages and productivity should not necessarily be associated with hard work.

For domestic industries not already co-opted by the global corporate cartels, their long term survival demands that automation be implemented to the greatest extent possible. Failure to do so might protect some jobs in the short term. However, in the longer term the loss of existing markets will inevitably lead to the loss of all jobs in that particular industry. The only alternative is the lowering of wages to the level of the overseas competition, an option no western worker wishes to contemplate. Consequently, the objectives of government policy should be to form partnerships that facilitate the earliest possible implementation of cybernetic automation and thereby deflect the momentum of these events to the public's advantage.

The socio-economic institutions existing in capitalist free-enterprise systems are generally not suited to the needs of a society whose production is based on cybernetics in that they offer few political mechanisms by which average people (particularly the structurally unemployed) could benefit directly. On the contrary, a widespread conversion to robotic industries has a high potential to create a large class of underprivileged citizens who have been displaced from their jobs.

In countries such as Sweden or Canada where free enterprise had been influenced to a certain extent by government intervention in the market place and also tempered by progressive social policies and programs, the political resistance to the social and economic imperatives of automation should be much less extreme than in a country like the US, The central problem to be faced is that family income has always been based on employment rather than on industrial output, a construct that has worked reasonably well to date. In a society dependent on robotics, industrial output will no longer be related to employment.

As long as the average unemployment rate remains relatively low, the structurally unemployed and the unemployable can be taken care of by the use of relatively modest unemployment insurance and welfare programs without creating the appearance of a major social problem. However, as the amount of unemployment increases, the standard of living provided by these programs will be found to be unacceptable to large numbers of workers who had once had average jobs in the manufacturing and service sectors. In the past, socially sympathetic political systems have delayed the introduction of technologies that would improve productivity at the expense of employment. In a cybernetic society, the political system, whether managed by the left, the center or the right, will be sorely tested in arranging an equitable distribution of wealth and maintaining a large and stable middle class. In fact the whole concept of a middle class would probably have to be re-examined.

Unions should be expected to press for a high degree of worker ownership in industries with a potential for automation and indeed this should be supported through government investment of public funds. The challenge will be to develop a public and industrial partnership to allow the maximum sharing of available work and wealth while still providing incentives and opportunities for people who are truly creative. The ownership of robotic industries by communities could very well be a more appropriate paradigm.

This is clearly an undertaking to be initiated before the pressures of international competition force it upon us. The longer we ignore the problem, the more difficult it will be to resolve. The current practice of providing government support to uncompetitive industries must be reexamined. One can always find good political, social and even short term economic reasons to justify the provision of such government support. However, regardless of the reasons for which the support is provided, it should be clearly identified as being of a temporary nature and it should be tied to a longer term plan to phase out or to automate that industry to the greatest possible extent.

It is ironic to think that the survival of free enterprise within western nations may very well depend on the public ownership of industry, though hopefully without state management.

If only we had *Al* and *Tabor* to help us clean up the mess.

Author

I am neither a financial, political nor social "Engineer" and make no claim to any expertise in these areas. I am a Mechanical Engineer and consider myself to be reasonably intelligent, and moderately aware. I sincerely believe that if it walks like a duck, quacks like a duck and looks like a duck, there is a very good chance that the item is in fact a duck.

This tale was prompted by my lack of patience with those who deny the obvious simply because they have no stomach for reality. Peter N. Brooks

Made in the USA
Lexington, KY
04 November 2010